Killers on Elm Street Part 3

Romell Tukes

Lock Down Publications and Ca$h
Presents
Killers on Elm Street 3
A Novel by *Romell Tukes*

Romell Tukes

Lock Down Publications
P.O. Box 944
Stockbridge, Ga 30281
www.lockdownpublications.com

Copyright 2021 Romell Tukes
Killers on Elm Street 3

First Edition June 2021
Printed in the United States of America

Lock Down Publications
Like our page on Facebook: Lock Down Publications @
www.facebook.com/lockdownpublications.ldp
Cover design and layout by: **Dynasty Cover Me**
Book interior design by: **Shawn Walker**
Edited by: **Jill Alicea**

Stay Connected with Us!

Text **LOCKDOWN** to 22828 to stay up-to-date with new releases, sneak peaks, contests and more...

Thank you!

Submission Guideline.

Submit the first three chapters of your completed manuscript to ldpsubmissions@gmail.com, subject line: Your book's title. The manuscript must be in a .doc file and sent as an attachment. Document should be in Times New Roman, double spaced and in size 12 font. Also, provide your synopsis and full contact information. If sending multiple submissions, they must each be in a separate email.

Have a story but no way to send it electronically? You can still submit to LDP/Ca$h Presents. Send in the first three chapters, written or typed, of your completed manuscript to:

LDP: Submissions Dept
P.O. Box 944
Stockbridge, Ga 30281

DO NOT send original manuscript. Must be a duplicate.

Provide your synopsis and a cover letter containing your full contact information.

Thanks for considering LDP and Ca$h Presents.

Acknowledgments

First and foremost, I would like to give all praises to The Most High Allah. Thanks to all my readers and followers. I'm only dropping the best. Shout to my family; shout to Yonkers and the whole 914; shout Moreno; YB, Ruff Ryders, Son God from M.V., OG Chuck from Brooklyn; shout to Armani Caesar from Buffalo, NY - I see you. Shout my guy Spice from Newburgh, NY. RIP to P-Cool from Hunts Point; BX; Casper from St. Louis and all my fallen soldiers. Shout to Lockdown Publications. The game is ours. We in the building and it's always a movie. All my books have a strong meaning and they all will have you out your seats. Thank you. Stay focused and full of good energy only. I'm on the way up.

Romell Tukes

Prologue
Staten Island, NY

Wolf looked at the rundown apartment, wondering what type of Mexican leader - or ex-Mexican leader - would even spend a night in this dump in the middle of the hood. Months ago, he had received this address from Ryan before his wife killed Ryan. He thought about Paola every night. He felt betrayed, lied to, used, and violated. Out of all people to kill, he found it crazy how his wife could kill his father cold-bloodedly with no remorse. Deep down he knew he was next, but Wolf was more than ready now. He thought about the night she had the gun to his face and all he could think about was what stopped her from killing him.

Wolf got out of the used Toyota and made his way into the building, which had a strong odor in the lobby, like a nursing home hallway.

Emilio's apartment was on the first floor at the end of the long hall. Wolf saw the apartment door was wide open with music playing in the backyard. It was Mazes Frankie Beverly "Can't Get Over You".

Wolf walked into the polished, clean apartment that was hooked up with new floor rugs, furniture, and fresh flowers everywhere. Nobody would ever imagine a crib this fancy in this rundown building, and that's why Emilio loved it.

Wolf saw a short Mexican man dancing in his living room with a glass of tequila in his hand. Emilio directed Wolf to take a seat while he was still two-stepping like he was in the club. Wolf had never seen an old Mexican nigga with so much swag. He wanted to laugh so badly while sitting down, but he kept his game face on because he needed answers.

Emilio eventually turned the music down and looked Wolf up and down. "So, you Wolf, huh?" Emilio asked, pouring himself another drink.

"Must have known I was coming?"

"You damn right. I know everything," Emilio said, finally sitting down, taking a deep breath. "Put your gun on the table," Emilio asked and Wolf did so with no complains.

"I got some questions."

"I know you do, but before we start, I want to play a little game as we go along with your questions and I will give you all facts." Emilio pulled out a .357 handgun, taking out the bullets and placing one in the chamber.

Wolf looked at him like he was crazy. He had no type of intentions to play with his life. This was literally suicide.

"No worries. I play alone. People always ruin the fun," Emilio said, smiling.

"First question."

"You only have five, so make them good," Emilio stated strongly, taking a sip of his tequila.

"Why do people want me dead?" Wolf asked. Emilio put the gun to his own head and pulled the trigger to get a click.

"Man, you wilding," Wolf said in shock because he thought he was faking.

"You're a piece to someone's missing puzzle. Someone has been pulling your strings since your sister's death, and now they see they can't use you no more. You're dead weight, just like how they did me."

"I don't understand?" Wolf said, not realizing he had just asked a second question.

Emilio placed the gun to his head again and pulled the trigger to feel the click.

"Aguilera had no clue the person who paid him to kill you knew all along you would sooner or later kill him. Aguilera and your person of interest used to fuck around until greed got in the way."

"So who is this fucking mystery person that's been trying get me killed and paying Mexican leaders to get me whacked?" Wolf asked the biggest question of his young life.

Emilio picked up the gun and pulled the trigger against his head to get another click, leaving Wolf's heart racing.

"Now this is the game changer, kid, because the person behind all of this is very powerful, rich, deadly, and sneaky. You would have never figured it out unless you came here. I was the one giving the money and word to send to the Five Families in Cali, but the person that wanted you and Ryan to kill each other must have got soft. Back in the day he would've killed his own father for money - which he did. Anyway, your own mother Rita is the one who set up everything. She is a powerful woman. She tried to have Ryan killed, but he killed her assassins and spared her life. Rita supplies the East Coast and down south with dope and coke. She did a good job at hiding it from you, Vic, and Black, but CB found out years ago, Wolf. Your mom won't stop until you're dead," Emilio said, seeing Wolf's amazed facial expression.

"Why would she kill my little sister? It don't make sense?" Wolf saw Emilio pick up the gun, putting it to his head.

Boom!

Emilio's blood splattered all over the walls and his body slumped onto the couch.

Wolf got his gun and tried to stand up, but his feet felt numb. He couldn't believe what he just heard. When he could move again, he left the apartment, trying to add everything up, because never in a million years would he think his mom was behind this. He hopped in his car, pulling off on a new mission.

Wolf grabbed his gun and got himself together. He knew if Emilio was willing to take his own life after releasing that information, then there was some truth to it, and it was deeper then he thought.

Once he made it outside, he tried to add everything up, but it was too much to calculate at once. Never in a million years would he think his mom was behind this.

Wolf looked up and down the pitch black block, feeling like someone was watching him, but he thought he was just tripping. He climbed into his Toyota, pulling off on a new mission.

Welcome back…

Chapter 1
Auburn Maximum Security Prison, NY

OG Chuck was on his way to his first visit in over ten years besides his legal visits, but he was certain that this wasn't a legal visit. He wore state green pants and an off-white collar shirt one of his young boys from Brooklyn gave him to wear. OG didn't know anything about designer clothes. He had been down almost two decades serving his life sentences. He wasn't expecting visitors, so he was excited for someone driving all the way up here to show some love and support.

As he walked through the long hallways, a couple of inmates shouted him out and he gave them a head nod. He wasn't into shaking hands and getting to affection. He was a real OG from Brooklyn and everybody respected him wherever he went because he demanded it. He was a man of respect and honor.

When he walked through the visit doors, he saw the visit room was half-empty, but when he saw a familiar face his smile turned into a frown. Looking at the beautiful brown-skinned woman with the bright hazel eyes who looked the same as she did twenty years ago brought old memories as he made his way to the table.

"What the fuck are you doing here? You got fucking nerve to bring your ass up here. After what the fuck you did, I should kill your ass," OG said, anger in his tone.

She rolled her eyes and took a deep breath. "Chuck, I'm sorry, but it's not what you think. I had to give you up or my children - our children - would have been in foster care somewhere. I had no choice."

"Bitch, you gave me up and you robbed me. The only reason why I didn't have your head handed to me was because of my children," he stated firmly, holding himself back from jumping over the table and slapping the shit out of her.

"You was up, Chuck. I built an empire off the little shit I took and you still have a lot left - especially in Cuba, I bet," she said, trying to make a point.

"That's not the point, Rita. The point is you snaked me to build your own empire and left me in prison."

"I said I was sorry, but I never told you to kill all those people," Rita said with a rude manner.

"Rita, I'ma give you ten seconds to tell me what the fuck you want, because I know you ain't come here to see how Im doing."

"Your daughter was killed. Your son was killed..."

"Hold up. If I find out you had anything to do with their deaths, I'ma have you chopped up into so many pieces you gonna look like ground beef, bitch," he said seriously, cutting her off.

"I would never kill my own children. Don't ever disrespect me like that."

"Hope not, for your sake."

"Your son will be home any day now and I just want to make sure you finally tell him you're his father. CB talks about you all the time and I want to tell him so bad, but I think it would be better if you do." Rita said.

"Don't tell him shit. I will tell him when the time is right," OG said, getting up to leave. "Don't ever come back. The only reason why I didn't spit in your face is because I don't want to go to the box today," OG said, leaving her sitting there.

***

OG walked back to his block, pissed off that Rita had the balls to bring her shady ass up and act like shit was cool after she put him in jail and took the stand at trial on him.

"OG, what's good, son? How was your visit?" CB asked, posted on the tier with two flunkies waiting for orders.

OG looked at CB for a minute without saying a word, wondering if he should tell him that he was his father.

"You good, old head?" CB asked, seeing he was zoned out.

"Yeah. An old friend came. It was cool. I'm about to take an old man nap. Hold my cell down and keep the noise down," OG said, going into his cell.

CB paid the grumpy old man no mind. CB had a week before he was released so he was on cloud nine, but only few people knew because in prison, telling someone you were going home was the worst mistake. CB saw niggas plant can tops and knives and niggas stab other niggas who had days to go home, so he learned from other people's mistakes not to talk too much.

***

Yonkers, NY

Wolf was relaxing in his condo in a nice area in Yonkers behind a middle school. He was watching the movie *Belly* on the 52-inch flat screen TV.

Since he had been back in New York, he had been laying low and focusing on putting a plan together. A couple of months ago he found out his mom was the face behind all the mayhem in Cali and Yonkers. He hadn't reached out to her yet because he needed a strong plan. If his mom was smart enough to set up everything, then he knew she had tricks up her sleeve.

When he killed his own brother Black a few months ago it crushed him, but now he wondered...if he would have kept him alive, could he have been of some help? But Wolf was against snitching.

Little did Wolf know Rita paid money to have Black killed, but the mission was aborted.

When Aguilera heard about the bounty on Black's head, he took it and sent Wolf to do the job, unaware Black was his brother. When Wolf got to the door in the pizza delivery uniform and saw it was Black, he made it seem like he was there to deliver pizza instead of killing him.

Wolf had plans to go meet Andy later, but he wanted to take a quick shower and nap after he looked at some porn. Sex was out of the picture because his wife was out to kill him next, and buying pussy wasn't a thought. He was too busy to go hunt some bitches just for some buns.

Killers on Elm Street 3

Romell Tukes

Chapter 2
Manhattan, NY

Paola was in her skyrise building in the penthouse, looking over the city at the bright tall buildings as she had been doing every night for the past couple of months. This was Paola's first time in New York and she loved it. Her crib was amazing: 12,179 square feet, four master bedrooms, three master walk-in bathrooms, two living rooms, upstairs and downstairs, private office, and a fully-stocked state of the art kitchen.

She was in her bedroom listening to a Chris Brown album, painting her toes in her silk robe with nothing underneath.

Paola had SUV's surrounding the building at all times protecting their boss. Paola had taken over the Five Families business with the blessing of her father and turned it into her own show. Now with power, money, and muscle, she had plans to take over New York, because Cali was already under her wing. That wasn't her only purpose in New York. She was here to find her husband and kill him if it was the last thing she did. Something she regretted regularly was not killing Wolf when she had the chance to because now she was on his turf. But she had more money and manpower than him, so she knew her advantage.

She was planning to go out tonight to a new club down the street she saw last week. Paola been partying and enjoying the city life because she knew any day could be her last, so she didn't let one go to waste.

"Oh my God, I hate thirsty niggas," she said to herself, seeing a gang of texts from a cute black dude she had met last week in a downtown club.

Since her marriage, she never took her wedding ring off for some reason only her heart knew. She couldn't deny the fact that she still loved Wolf, but he had to pay the price for what he had done to her family.

***

Washington Heights, NY

Salma wore a nice sundress and heels on the hottest day of the summer. Her hair was in a bun, showing her beautiful Puerto-Rican features. She stood in the back of some buildings on Dychman with six big Spanish guards, waiting for her men to come back with a surprise for her.

This was home for her and the crew she had built from the ground up. Salma was one of the most powerful woman in New York. She called her crew the Puerto Rican Mafia because of how they put in work and sell tons of keys all over the Tri-state and PR.

Salma wanted answers for her lover Ryan's death and she wasn't going to stop until she got them. Her focus right now was finding Ryan's son Wolf, but he was nowhere to be found. She had a lead on him when he first came back to New York and landed at the JFK airport. She even followed him to Emilio's home in Staten Island. At that time she had no clue what was going on, but when Wolf left Emilio's crib, she went inside to find Emilio dead. She knew who he was, but she thought he was dead or a ghost.

"Here they come, boss," one of her guards said, seeing three goons drag a man into the back with a pillowcase around his head.

The man was tossed at her feet. He was trying to get loose, but the restraints were too tight on his wrist and ankles.

Salma pulled the pillowcase over his head to see small dreads. The man was Jamaican.

"What the fuck is this?" Salma asked her goons.

"He's the one who had a bounty on Wolf's head, so we picked him up," one of the goons said, shrugging his shoulders.

"Okay." The Jamaican's eyes were wide and red. Salma snatched the duct tape from around his mouth and stared at him. "How do you know Wolf, and where can I find him?" she asked in her sweet, calm voice.

The Jamaican nigga was lost in her beauty and blue eyes. He somewhat was stuck until she forced her gun into his mouth.

"My boss wants Wolf and Andy dead because Wolf killed his connect, and Andy killed his brother a couple of years back," the man said with a Jamaican accent.

"Who the fuck is your boss?" she asked, squatting down, seeing him breaking his neck to look under her dress.

"Mad Max from Brooklyn," he said.

Salma looked at her goons and they all looked at each other. They had never heard of him before.

"So he paid two million dollars to have both men killed?"

"No, two million apiece," he corrected her

"He must really want him dead. But they have to get through me first because I'm looking for him also and when I'm done, they can do as they please with him."

"Mad Max is a dangerous man," the man said with fear in his voice.

"Ain't we all? Where can I find Wolf?"

"In Yonkers. He's hidden out somewhere. But if you can find Andy, you can find him, from my understanding. But they are deadly, I must warn you," he stated.

"Well, thank you."

Boom! Boom!

"Send the homies to take care of him," Salma said in Spanish, pointing at the Jamaican's dead body.

***

Downtown Yonkers

Andy had opened a tea shop in the busy area of Yonkers. All you saw was white people coming and going to work.

Andy was in his small office taking thirty bricks of coke out of the safe under the floor for his homie Force to come pick up in minutes.

Life had been fine for Andy since losing his grandmother, his father, his girl Erica, and his best friend Smurf. Killing Lingo was the hardest task he was ever put up against, but he did it, and Wolf killing Black was the icing on the cake.

The city of Yonkers had been quiet these past couple of months until recently, when he heard a gang of Jamaicans had come looking for him and Wolf.

Andy's young boys ended up in a shootout, leaving five Jamaicans dead and two of his people dead. This event took place last week. Andy had no clue who was behind it, but he had his people on it. He had a strong feeling something big was about to go down and he wanted to know what he was up against.

When he told Wolf, the response he got was different than what he was used to: a laugh. Wolf told him sometimes you had to go back to the basics just to build a bigger foundation. Andy had no clue what he meant, but he agreed. Wolf told him soon some people would be looking for him and they needed an army. Andy told him that was already covered. He had the whole city under his finger.

Andy's connect Trigger was back in New York. He had to make an appointment because he was running out of work. He still cut Wolf 50/50 because without him, he wouldn't be in his position. Now he was trying to put his little niggas on.

Chapter 3

Somers, NY

Bella was having a one-on-one with one of the kids at her new job she had been at for five months now. She was a counselor in a detention center for the youth. When Bella was released from rehab, she found out her friend Christina died from an overdose on heroin. Bella was shocked and hurt. She blamed herself for not taking action and bringing her along with her to rehab. Bella came out of rehab clean, focused, and glowing, looking like her old self.

While in her rehab treatment, she received the worst news from an anonymous messenger, who delivered her a folder full of photos and a tape recorder. Looking through the pics, she saw Wolf leaving her father's house seconds after he was killed, but what broke the ice was Wolf on a tape recorder. Wolf and Aguilera were talking and everything was exposed. Bella was shocked. She had no idea Wolf was a killer. Even after the night she saw him kill her partner when she was on duty as a cop in Yonkers, she gave him the benefit of the doubt.

Hearing him pull the trigger and killing her father hurt her worse than his death, but she believed in karma. Any love she did have for him was gone. She hated him. Bella always had a deep secret that she never had a chance to tell Wolf. When they met at NYU, she was the one who told her father about him and how she thought he would be useful to him. Bella knew what her father was into, but little did she know Wolf was already the chosen one.

The first day she got out of rehab, she went to check her bank account to see how much money she had saved up from cleaning floors in the rehab center. She remembered it was close to five hundred dollars. But when she went to Chase bank, the clerk told her she had $150,000 in her account. She was so overwhelmed that she made the clerk check twice just in case it was a scam or typo. Bella took all the money out of the bank and went to buy a car and an apartment in a nice area called Sleepy Hollow because she was homeless.

Luckily she was able to land a good job, thanks to her Criminal Justice degree. Life was great for her, but she needed to go out and have fun, so this weekend she planned to go out to a new lounge in Harlem called Zip Code.

***

Harlem, NY

The lounge was full of beautiful women and men enjoying themselves and mingling, listening to the soft R & B music play in the background. The bar was packed and the bottle girls were running upstairs and downstairs all night pleasing the partygoers. There was a strict dress code, no boots, no sneakers, and no hats. Most people were dressed to impress in designer outfits, making a fashion statement.

"Welcome home, bro," Rell told CB, who was sipping on a glass of Remy, his favorite drink.

"Good looks, boy. This spot is my type of vibe. A nigga too old to be in some wild club type shit," CB said.

"Yeah, this some grown man shit, Blood," Rell, said drinking Dom P like it was water.

CB had come home from prison yesterday and his mom Rita was there to pick him up in an all candy red Bentley Continental GT W12, which was his welcome home gift, along with a condo outside of Yonkers. Rita also gave him $700,000 for pocket change and told him in a matter of days she would be sending him a bus load of keys. She had a real school bus she drove as a job, but used it to traffic drugs. For years she had been doing it while the kids were at school.

"I'ma have something big for you, bro. Facts. You kept it solid since I met you, fam," CB told his man, who had been with him since day one of his long bid.

CB and Rell grew up together in Yonkers on Elm Street, but Rell recently moved to Newburgh with his baby mother Orianna, who was from Newburgh.

"Say less, bro. You already know how we do." Rell saw a bad Spanish bitch at the bar staring into their section. "I think shawty on your line, bro," Rell told CB, who met eyes with the dime bitch in the white slit dress and long hair in a ponytail.

"Damn, Blood, she fire. Let me see if I still got it, son," CB said, standing up, fixing his Dior outfit. CB had his long braids swimming down his back, a fresh shape up, and his handsome face that drove women insane. Once at the bar, CB saw an empty stool next to the Spanish mami.

"Excuse me, can I get you a drink?" CB asked her as she turned around to look at him. CB was fucked up by her blue and greenish eyes that matched with her very light skin making her look white. CB saw her big titties and her ass hanging off the stool in her tight dress.

I'm okay. I got a Long Island Iced Tea," she replied with a smile, very respectfully. She liked what she saw. He was tall, stocky, and had long hair, the pretty boy type of nigga.

"Can we get the next one on me, please?"

"Well, since you said please, why not?" she said, letting him order two rounds of Long Island Iced Tea.

"Where you from?"

"America...how about you?" she said, laughing.

"Funny. I'm from Yonkers." When CB said Yonkers, he saw a sour look on her face. "Guess you been there."

"A couple of times, but I'm from Sleepy Hollow."

"Oh, you close. What's your name?" he asked.

"Isabella."

"That fits you well," CB said, taking a sip of the drink, not liking how sweet it was.

"What's yours?"

"CB."

"I'm sure that's not your birth name."

"It's Prince, but only someone special can call me that."

"I'll stick with CB for now, papi. You look Spanish?" Isabella asked, looking into his brown eyes and then at his good hair.

"I'm mixed with all types of shit, ma. How about you?"

"Puerto Rican," she said, getting hyped, dancing to the old Big Pun song playing in the background.

"Okay. You single?"

"Like a dollar bill, papi. How about you? And don't lie to me. I hate liars" Isabella said, seriously feeling tipsy.

"I'm single. I just came home from prison, so I'm trying to get my life in order."

"Okay. I don't judge. It's sad if you had to do a bid by yourself, but welcome home. Cheers to that," she said as they tipped glasses.

CB saw every nigga in the club staring at Isabella because she was eye candy. She was the type of woman most niggas would be too scared to approach because her beauty was strong, powerful, alluring, and fearsome.

"I have to go. My friend has to get home. Do you think we can meet up sometime?" CB asked

"I don't see why not," she replied, exchanging numbers with him, hoping he was worth her time.

Chapter 4

Coney Island, Brooklyn

Maryanna was dining at an amazing seafood restaurant on the long strip full of restaurants and boardwalks for tourists to look at the beautiful sandy beach across the street from the restaurant. It was a nice summer day and she was going to enjoy it. She was alone, as always. She hated to be under or around people all day. It was her own little pet peeve since she had been a kid.

Maryanna was in New York on a manhunt for a couple of targets, but her number one was the bitch who killed her brother Ryan. Maryanna lived in the Dominican Republic but she had been back and forth from New York to DR her whole life.

She was so sexy. She looked painted. She took good care of herself, making her look forever eighteen with a killer body. She was very wealthy and not because of drugs. Her grandfather was a millionaire and left her everything, millions of dollars and close to sixty real estate properties. Her brother was left nothing because he killed their father for the love of money. That's when he and Maryanna fell out.

Maryanna had plans to kill Ryan one day, but someone beat her to the punch, so she was really upset about that. She was well-trained, better than Ryan, because her teachers were Brazilian martial arts, masters who were not only in fighting but in shooting also. She was very disciplined, shapely, and swift, but her beauty could decoy and bait in anybody who laid eyes on her.

Maryanna used to bring Wolf to DR to train when he was a kid and teenager with the best of the best. She made him swear to never tell anybody what he would do when he came to live with her in the summer. It was their little secret. Wolf almost became as good as her, but she knew Wolf's heart wasn't into killing. When she got word Wolf was in Cali causing hell, she knew her hard work had paid off and she was proud of her nephew.

She hadn't seen Wolf since he was eighteen years old, but one thing she knew for sure was that she would be seeing him sooner rather than later.

***

Gunhill, Bronx

"Where these niggas think they at, bro, Jamaica? Walking around the yard barefoot drinking Jamaican rum," Demon said, watching a group of Rastas smoke and drink in a backyard of a small brick house on a corner of a four-way street.

Force and Demon were best friends from Yonkers on Elm Street, where they both grew up in poverty in the same building. Force was moving keys for Andy, his mentor, in the hood, but Force had his own crew of young killers and Demon was the top gunner.

Demon was seventeen years old and a vicious gunslinger. He was short and cocky with an evil attitude. He sold his soul to the devil when he was thirteen and after that, he became a madman. He had three sixes tattooed on his face under his right eye on his dark skin, which made it hard to see from a distance. He had natural amber/gray eyes from his grandmother, who was Haitian.

"He's on the move, going back in the house, bro," Demon stated.

Force watched the nigga they called Chance from Brooklyn leave the house with a thick dark-skinned bald-headed bitch with a phat ass, climbing in a black Mercedes AMG C63 coupe with tints and rims.

"Perfect," Demon said, blowing smoke out of his nose and mouth. It wasn't weed smoke. Demon smoked wet, a.k.a. PCP, like niggas smoked cigarettes.

"Bro, roll the window down when you smoke that shit around me!" Force yelled at Demon because he hated the strong black marker smell.

"My bad, son, damn."

"It's 12:30 a.m. and this nigga pulling into a park," Force said, keeping a distance on the Benz, watching it park near the bathroom. Force parked his black Camaro at the end next to a large green dumpster so he couldn't be seen.

***

"Ohhhh yesssss!" the dark-skinned woman yelled while riding Chance's dick in his driver seat. This was her first time fucking in a Benz, so she was extra wet. She had met Chance earlier today at her girl's house. She told Chance everything about her except that she was a minor, only sixteen.

"Damn, your pussy tight," Chance moaned, going deeper in her walls while sucking on her hard nipples and little breasts. Chance came inside of her while she danced on his dick.

"Ugghhh, fuck, it's too big. You're hurting me," she said, grinding on his pole.

Bloc! Bloc! Bloc! Bloc! Bloc!

The windows to the Benz shattered all over the young girl's dead body. Chance got out of the car crawling to see four feet standing in front of him.

"Where you going, buddy?" Force asked him.

"What's going on?"

"We want to know who you work for. Who you sent to Yonkers to kill my man? Because we got wind it was you, boy?" Force asked.

"It was an order from Mad Max. You killed his brother Zion who was living in Mount Vernon a while back and Wolf killed his plug, which I don't know nothing about," Chance said, shaking in his boots.

"Where can I find him?"

"He's underground in Brooklyn. He has a big army in Brooklyn. Mad Max runs the Shower Posse with a crew of killers in the States and his father runs Jamaica. He's nothing to fuck with, mon," Chance said in a deep Jamaican accent.

"Damn, son, this nigga about to give us his Social Security number any second," Demon said.

Force put three holes in his head like a bowling ball before walking off.

Chapter 5

Brooklyn, NY

Mad Max was in the back of his meat store watching the soccer game on his large flat screen TV with a couple of his goons, smoking and drinking.

Mad Max had been born in Kingston, Jamaica. His family started a crew of drug lords who crowned themselves as the infamous Shower Posse and his father and mother were the original members and still were. Growing up with six brothers and seven sisters in a wealthy family, his destiny was already chosen for him. Mad Max and his brother Zion moved to the states at a young age to expand their family network. While Zion controlled Mount Vernon, the Bronx, and Yonkers, Mad Max controlled Brooklyn and the rest of the New York City drug trade. They both had very few clients because they didn't trust Americans.

When Andy killed Zion, it hit Mad Max hard because he loved his little brother and he had always looked after him since they were kids, so he took Zion's loss personally. Mad Max paid big money to find out who was responsible for Zion's murder. He found a chick named Shontell, a dancer. Shontell told him Andy was a regular at the club and he was asking a lot of questions about Zion the night of his death. Shontell also told Mad Max she knew Andy was a well-known stick-up kid. The only thing she didn't tell Mad Max was she was the one who set up the whole lick. Shontell was Andy's best friend Smurf's wifey, but she was out for herself. Unfortunately, she was murdered just like Smurf.

Mad Max wanted Wolf for other reasons. He killed Mad Max's heroin plug, Jimenez, and at the time he was killed, he owed Mad Max 20 million dollars' worth of dope. Mad Max's wife was Nannie, a beautiful mixed Latin woman who was the daughter of Jimenez. Not many people knew Jimenez had children and he tried his best at keeping Nannie a secret. Mad Max met his wife in Jamaica years ago and it was love at first sight. The two had been together ever since and had two beautiful daughters. Mad Max was tall, lean, and handsome, with long thick dreads and gold teeth. He wore a lot of jewelry, just like his father and brothers. He had Brooklyn on his back, especially the Flatbush and Bed-Stuy area where he grew up.

"Mad Max!" one of his guards shouted, walking into the back with a phone in his hand.

"What?"

"They just found Chance's body in a park in the Bronx," his guard stated.

"Blood clot! Come on," Mad Max said, getting up, pissed he had to cut his soccer game short.

***

Hollywood, Cali

Paola's mom had just come back to one of her mansions after shopping on Rodeo Drive. She placed her bags in the living room. She looked sexy in her minidress and heels, showing a lot of skin to attract men, which was too easy. She was freaky, into orgies and swinger parties.

"Jenn! Jenn!" she yelled, looking for her maid so she could make dinner for two because she was having company tonight. She had just met a young handsome black dude and she was in the mood for some good love-making tonight. "Oh my God!" she screamed, seeing Jenn's dead body lying across the counter neatly face down.

"Don't look so surprised," Julie said, walking out of a closet to see Paola's mom in tears and covering her mouth.

"Why? Julie, why?"

"That's the question everybody wants to know. Why did your husband Ruiz kill my family? Why did you fuck my husband?" Julie asked, catching her off-guard with her remark.

"What is this about me fucking your husband? The dick was trash anyway."

"I agree. But I'm here for Paola."

"She is in New York. I don't have nothing to do with y'all beef or problems."

"That's good to know, but you're just the messenger," Julie said, shooting her six times in her upper chest, watching her fall back into the sink and then drop to the floor.

Julie walked out of the crib in a black satin Fendi dress, looking like she was going to a photo shoot. Her goons were parked a block away on the hill in a SUV, waiting on their boss.

There was only one thing on Julie's mind, and that was taking control of the Cali drug trade. The only person stopping her was Paola, who had taken over the Five Families operations. Julie had been waiting on her time to shine for years. She put in too much work to let some little bitch snatch it from her. After Julie killed her husband Sousa with the help of Ryan, her secret lover, and his son Wolf, she built her own army with the help of a couple of Blackhands, Mexican leaders.   She had plans to go to New York and complete her mission, and nothing was going to stop her.

***

Yonkers, NY

Wolf was sitting at the waterfront feeding the ducks and birds bread, enjoying his morning, getting peace of mind. It always seems like if it wasn't one problem, then it was another in his life. He now had to worry about some Jamaicans he had never seen or never heard of, but Andy said his people were going to handle it.

"Can I join? It's such a beautiful morning," a female voice said from behind him.

Wolf as he turned around to see how sexy she was. His dick got hard, but he controlled his lust. "My pleasure," Wolf said, moving over so she could sit down.

"Thanks. You ever watch the ocean waves and realize how the wind always directs the waves in one direction?"

"Langston Hughes, 'The Dream Keeper', 1932," Wolf stated. He knew the poem by heart.

"Smart, just like your father."

"Excuse me?" Wolf said, now looking into her blue eyes.

"Wolf, I have been looking for you and I must admit, you're a hard person to find."

"If you're going to kill me, time is money," he replied, making her laugh.

"No. I'm not the enemy, Wolf. I'm more so on your side. I'm just trying to find out who killed Ryan."

"Why does it matter to you?"

"He was my heart and the only man I ever loved. He talked so much about you."

"You're the woman who used to meet him in Vegas?"

"Yes. I'm Salma."

"I know who you are and why you're here, Salma Aguilera, but it won't take long for you to find out who killed him. You found me in the nick of time, thanks to the Jamaicans. But I have to go, Have a nice day," Wolf said, walking away.

Chapter 6

Manhattan, NY

Paola used the five star fancy hotel bar and restaurant to hold meetings in, and today she was meeting with her father Ruiz's biggest client. Nine guards were seated throughout the area, keeping a close eye on Paola. Since taking over the family business, she had been running wild because she took over all Five Families clients. Her brother was in Cali taking care of the West Coast affairs.

Paola received the news of her mother's death and she was hurt by it. She had no clue who was behind the attack, but she was going to find out.

Her guest walked inside the restaurant with a crew all armed with weapons, making Paola goons get on alert.

"Good evening," Paola said, standing to shake her guest's hands.

"Nice to meet you. This is my son, CB." She smiled at her. "Your dress fits you beautifully. Now I see why Ruiz spoke highly of you," Rita said. She was looking beautiful herself with her hair flat and hanging down to her shoulders.

"I hope he did, and likewise. I hope we can build a good business connection because I hear you got New York in a chokehold – well, at least certain areas."

"I do, but I have a lot of opponents. I plan to take over the whole city slowly but surely," Rita said, drinking water out of a glass.

"Let me know if I can be any help. I will be supplying you the coke for the same price you been getting it for and I will make sure you're getting the purest coke," Paola stated, looking at CB stare at her like she was a piece of meat. He was starting to freak her out.

"Perfect, Paola. I will have different pick up spots every shipment"

"Great."

"Are you married?"

"Huh?" Paola asked, looking at her wedding ring, forgetting she always wore it. "Oh, yeah, this old thing… I'm divorced," Paola said, playing with the ring.

"Ohhh, I'm so sorry! You look so young," Rita stated.

"It's life. I have to go to Queens for another meeting. Be ready tomorrow. My men will be waiting for you."

"Okay, thank you for everything. I love to see women in power," Rita said before leaving.

CB took one last look at Paola and felt his dick jump. He had never seen a bitch so bad in his life. He wanted her, but he could tell she was way outta his league. He was a worker for his mom and Paola was a boss. It didn't add up.

***

Yonkers, NY

"Bro, this little nigga is the new Smurf. He got heavy respect in these streets. I'm telling you, son, this kid is the real deal," Andy told Wolf while they were standing in a Pizza Hut parking lot.

"Okay, I believe you."

"Good. He been waiting to tell me something, but I was Upstate." Andy saw a Camaro SS race into the parking lot blasting the new Casanova album.

Force parked between the two luxury cars and got out with a blunt hanging from his lips.

"Yooo, what's good, son?" Force said, embracing Andy and looking at the infamous Wolf. Force looked at Wolf and he would never guess he was looking at a real live killer.

"This is Wolf, the bro," Andy said, introducing the two men.

"Your name is a ghost out here, son. We heard a lot about you - Elm Street's finest," Force said, tossing his blunt on the ground.

"That's what's up. I heard you got some important information?" Wolf asked, getting straight to the point because it was starting to rain.

"Facts, I dug deeper into this Jamaica shit and Mad Max is their leader. He wants to kill you, Wolf. The reason behind it is his plug was a man named Jimenez, but I believe it's deeper," Force said.

"Jimenez, huh? Okay, and why does he want him?" Wolf said, pointing at Andy.

"He killed his brother a while back. Me and Demon are trying to locate Mad Max now in BK, but were having a hard time," Force stated.

"If I get time, I can help," Wolf stated before Andy cut Wolf off.

"You can handle it. If we need to step in, we will, but you have a hundred man army, Force. You're not a soldier no more. You're a leader." Andy walked off with Wolf, leaving Force in his own thoughts

***

San Quentin Prison, Cali

Ruiz sat on his bed reading the Quran, taking his time. Ruiz read the Bible and the Torah also. He liked to understand all religions to compare them.

Today an inmate on death row was executed so inmates banged on their cell bars, yelling and screaming.   Ruiz said a prayer for the man because he knew his days were coming sooner rather than later.

Since all the other families of the Five Families were dead because of Ryan and Wolf, he gave his empire to his daughter, Paola, and she was doing an amazing job at taking over.   He thought it was too soon for her to go up to New York to open up shop, but he knew she wanted blood. The death of his wife almost left him in tears, but he knew she had her days numbered because she was a dirtbag.

Ruiz took his glasses off and laid back on his bunk, daydreaming about the 60's, 70's, and 80's when he was the man and killing anybody that got in his way, including family and friends.

Chapter 7

Newburgh, NY

"Oooohhh, shit! Gurl, fuck that dick, bitch!" Rell moaned. He was in his bedroom listening to the group 112's album *Room 112*, which was Orianna's favorite.

Determined to fuck her man's brains out, she rode his dick hard like a wild cowgirl, making sexy fuck faces, turning him on.

"Ummmm, yessss, daddy!" Orianna moaned in ecstasy, holding his hands, which were spread out behind his head.

"I'm cumming!" Rell screamed.

She rolled her hips on his dick like a wild animal until she felt him fill her small pussy up with cum.

Orianna was honey-complexioned eye candy. She was petite, but she was a beast in the bed. Her curly brown hair, hazel eyes, thick lips, and perfect jawline and nose made niggas flock to her feet. She was a dance instructor at a college nearby, which she also attended.

She climbed below Rell's towards his semi-hard dick and eased it into her wet mouth, slowly sucking on the head. She slid her head up and down, taking inch by inch down her long throat.

"Damn, bae," Rell moaned, curling his toes as she forced his dick down her throat, increasing the suction on the dick, making him feel like crying.

Orianna bopped up and down on his dick, getting it wet and sloppy. She was slurping on his pre-cum, having fun before she stopped because she knew any second he was going to cum.

"Fuck this pussy, nigga," she said, laying on her back, opening her legs wide.

Rell saw her small, pretty shaved pussy with creamy cum dripping out. He entered her tight pussy, trying to stretch open her walls going deeper into her warmness.

"Uhhhhh fuckkk!" she screamed in pleasure and pain because her little body could only easily take a dick under five inches. She was only 4'11" and 110 pounds so she was fragile.

The pussy was so good that Rell wanted to stay in her love box forever. She tried to pull back, but Rell thrust his hips into her pussy, driving her crazy. Rell came deep inside of her as his body jerked with the ugliest face she had ever seen. She felt her own orgasm before he pulled out of her slippery walls and saw his dick coated with cream that could pass for whipped cream.

"I have to take a shower and go to school or I'ma be late," Orianna said, jumping out of the bed, seeing it was close to 10:00 a.m.

"I gotta go to Yonkers anyway," Rell said, seeing five new texts from CB telling him it was time.

Rell was a very handsome young brother: dark-skinned, chiseled, six feet tall, two hundred pounds lean with cuts, waves, chinky eyes, a chipped tooth in a nice smile, and he had big Shaq hands.

When CB was gone, Rell did everything he could do to remain above water: working 9 to 5 jobs, selling weed, crack, and even bootleg clothes. When he met Orianna, she was with her ex-boyfriend Spice, who was doing time in prison. Rell had never seen the dude, but his name was big in Newburgh. Rell heard he was up moving weight in the hood from Orianna, who talked about him daily.

He got dressed and left the crib to go get his daughter from his mom's house to take her to daycare.

***

Lower East Side

Andy was at a massage parlor, waiting on his time to get a body rub by a beautiful Thailand woman. He had been coming here for two months because it was a big stress reliever for him.

Andy was playing on his iPhone, scrolling through the pictures of a couple of Instagram model bitches he had fucked for a couple of hundreds of dollars. He hated how bitches were on the 'gram trying to look all sexy but when you saw them in person, they looked like hoodrats with bald heads and fake eyelashes.

A Spanish woman was coming out from the back saying goodbye to the foreign woman in their Thai language. When Andy saw the woman's sexy legs and body he got stuck, but when he saw her face up close, he recognized her.

"Excuse me, I find it rude how someone will be able to conversate with a person and give them the wrong number," Andy stated. The woman looked at him, smiling, remembering him from months ago coming out of a lawyer's building.

"I see you never forget a face," Maryanna said.

"I also never forget a name, and since you never gave it to me, I hope you will now. I believe in destiny and me seeing you here only makes me believe we're made for each other," Andy said seriously.

"You're so cute, papi, but I'm maybe out of your bracket," she said in her Dominican accent.

"Maybe you're just all talk and scared of a real man who's really going to put that dick down on you," Andy said, getting up and walking to the back for his massage.

Maryanna was dumbfounded and turned on like never before.

An hour later, Andy felt like a new man. His body and mind were relaxed. He made it out to his Benz to see a small note on his windshield.

"Hey handsome papi, my name is Maryanna from D.R. this is my real number I would like to see more of you and that dick game better be on point. Call me."

Andy started dancing in the middle of the street, almost getting hit by four cabs back to back. He was unaware that Maryanna was watching him and laughing.

Romell Tukes

Chapter 8

Atlanta, GA

Trigger had just left his Atlanta condo in his Wraith. He was on his way to Atlanta International Airport to catch a flight to New York to go meet with his plug and see what was so important. Trigger had been in Atlanta for almost five years now in zone 6, trapping hard. He was one of the biggest plugs out there. He was twenty-nine, pushing thirty in a couple of days, born and raised in Yonkers, NY on Elm Street. His little brother Lil Tom was killed a few years back while he was dealing with Andy and Smurf.

Atlanta was a new beginning for Trigger when he came home from prison. He met a bad stripper bitch on a jail dating site, moved to Atlanta with her, and started chasing a big bag. The stripper bitch ended up getting killed in a club parking lot shootout with Trigger and some hating niggas from zone 3 trying to rob him, but he ended up killing three of them. The club had no cameras and no witnesses came forward, so Trigger ended up getting away with it and making a name for himself, then forming his own crew.

Trigger whipped the Wraith through the hot Atlanta streets of downtown. The only thing he disliked about the city was the heavy gay population because there were times he would see bad thick, sexy dime pieces, thinking they were women but they were transgenders.

It didn't take long for him to arrive at the airport. He saw women staring at him in the Wraith as he cruised with the top down. Trigger was a *GQ* type of nigga, so women flocked to him. He was tall at 6'5", muscular, with a goatee, butter pecan skin, and tattooed up. Most women thought he was an NBA player instead of a trap star. He hadn't been to NY in years, so he only hoped no BS went on.

***

Newburgh, NY

"Spice, what's the word, son? What's poppin' for tonight?" Sticks asked, drinking a cup of lean in a Sprite bottle at 10 a.m.

"Nigga, whatever the day brings, fam," Spice said, leaning on his Audi i8, watching his block do big numbers as fiends raced up and down the strip.

Spice was clocking big money and he had a crew of killers on speed dial. He was feeding his whole hood, especially Dubicus and Liberty. He was still dealing with Andy and putting his money with his so they could get shit from Trigger in Atlanta.

Spice had cribs in Newburgh, Yonkers, and Brooklyn. He was moving around every day and networking to build his empire.

Looking at his phone, he couldn't help but smile when he saw the text from Orianna telling him she was trying to suck his dick and fuck him in his car before she got to work because her man was outta town. Spice didn't even reply because he had other shit to do, but her pussy and head game were fire. He had been fucking her for years. He didn't care about her boyfriend Rell. He was a nobody to him. Three days ago, Spice and his boys ran a train on Orianna and after that, he lost respect for her.

"Ay yo, Spice, let me get some money" a little thot named Tee Tee asked. He used to fuck her back in the day until coke fucked her life up.

"Bitch, you better cash out that EBT card," Spice said, laughing, climbing in his car with his little shooter sticks.

"That's why I burnt your ass back in the day," she mumbled under her breath, walking off.

***

New York City, NY

Audrey walked past Times Square, sightseeing, enjoying the beautiful city. New York was a long way from home, but she had her reasons. She was looking for the man who killed her father Cruz, who was a respected member of the Five Families. When Wolf and

Ryan murdered her dad, she felt like her soul was snatched from her because she was a daddy's girl.

Audrey was a pro at hunting people down and she had the best help, which was a hacker she had been in the Marines with. Audrey was a skilled shooter, killer, and fighter.

She wore a hat, sunglasses, jeans, and a shirt, trying to conceal her true beauty because New York dudes were good at harassing her and any other female. In a couple of hours when night hit, she had plans to go to Yonkers and check out a couple of locations her friend gave her on Wolf.

***

Cross County, Yonkers

CB lived in the nice middle class area outside of Yonkers in a hooked-up three bedroom apartment fit for a king. Tonight was a special night because he had company over and she was looking so good he couldn't even focus.

This was CB and Bella's second date and she was feeling his vibes, so she agreed to come over to his place for dinner. The takeout food was amazing from Red Lobster. They were both well past full.

"Thanks. You really know what to order since you can't cook, but next time, let me do the cooking," Isabella said, following him onto his thick carpeted living room barefoot.

"Glad there will be a next time, because I'm feeling you," CB said, looking into her beautiful eyes, then at her breasts busting out her dress almost seeing her nipples.

"I feel comfortable around you and since I told you about my addiction, I feel like you accept me for me, so that means a lot," Isabella said, seriously. She was really feeling him, but she didn't want to get hurt or hurt him because he was a good man.

"I'm trying to make you wifey."

"Oh, is that right? Well, let's just see where it goes," she said, lying on his lap on the couch as they watched a Kevin Hart movie and then fell asleep on each other.

Chapter 9

Chelsea, NY

Roger left his office in his skyrise building, headed home to his 20.4 million dollar mansion in Long Island where he came from a wealthy affluent family. After graduating from Harvard University, Roger opened his own insurance company and became one of the biggest insurance companies in New York. Roger was a man who always wanted more so he found another lane that made him millions of dollars. Roger had a lot of rich buddies that loved coke and crack, but they couldn't risk their position by going to the slums to cop weight and end up in jail or snitched on. That's where Roger came in. He was buying bricks at 25k a piece from Rita, his longtime friend, and selling them for 40k a piece. He had rich clients who never copped less than twenty keys at once so he was making lots of money to support his own luxurious lifestyle, which was gambling, yachts, golfing, partying, and big vacations with beautiful women.

The elevator stopped at the lower garage level where his 650 Mercedes-Maybach with curtains in the windows was parked. He had a personal driver that drove him around all day and he got paid a six figure salary. Roger climbed in the back, wondering why his driver didn't open the door for him as he normally did.

"Mike, I'm ready," Roger said, texting on his phone, waiting for the car to start up. Roger looked up to see Mike's head slumped in his seat with five holes in his head. When Roger saw this he screamed and opened the door to run and get security upstairs in the lobby, but a man dressed in all black with a pistol in his hand slid into the backseat with him.

"Where you going, bud? We have to talk, and depending how it goes, you may end up like your friend in the front seat," Wolf stated, pointing the gun at Roger seeing him sweat.

"Whatever you want. Just don't hurt me please!" Roger begged

"Good. What's your connection to Rita?"

"To who?"

Psst!

"Ahhhhhhhhh!" Roger yelled in pain after getting shot in the kneecap.

"Let's try this again, bro."

"Okay! She is my plug! I pay 25,000 for a key. I cop 300-600 keys a month from her."

"Who else you know she sell to?"

"Some mobsters in Brooklyn and a lot of upper class powerful people. She is a connected woman. I think you're outta your league. She will have you dead within hours," Roger said, holding his knee and crying.

"I'll handle her when the time comes. When was your last shipment?"

"Yesterday. A light-skinned kid I had never seen before dropped it off to me".

"What was his name?"

"CB, I believe."

"Damn!" Wolf shouted, not knowing his brother was home.

"Do yourself a favor and let it go. I'm telling you, this bitch is the real deal."

"I believe you, and I'll be the judge of that. But today you will meet your Judgement Day."

Wolf shot him twice in the head with his Glock 9mm with a silencer attached to it. Wolf hopped out and went to his BMW, on a new mission.

***

South Central, Cali

Mario watched his truck movers unload a new shipment of coke and heroin. He owned a truck company, but he used that as a front to move his drugs in and out of state all over the west coast. In a matter of months, Mario became a boss under his sister, who was in New York trying to network and open shop. Mario knew what she was really up there for, and that was Wolf. Mario thought it was a bad idea to case Wolf to kill him because he was smart and very dangerous. Mario knew that firsthand because Wolf saved his life, killing five men and not breaking a sweat like he was some type of killing machine.

Mario was now focused on money and rebuilding his father's empire and he was doing a good job. The death of his mother hit him hard. He just recently buried her and it was the saddest day of his life.

Mario had an army of MS-13 with him and they were on the hunt for his mom's killer. Mario recently became a Blackhead member so he was calling shots in South Central and LA.

***

Bronx, NY

Andy was waiting at the car dealership his man owned to change cars, which he did daily now just in case the Feds were on his line. While waiting on his all-red Aston Martin Valhalla with the twin turbo V6 engine worth 1.5 million, he saw a bad Spanish bitch walking to a Rolls Royce Wraith Black Badge Coupe fresh off the floor.

"Damn, ma," Andy said loud enough so she could hear.

The woman turned around to see Andy looking at her and she rolled her eyes before climbing in the driver's seat of the luxury car with the top off.

Andy saw how her wide phat ass jiggled in her shorts. She was short with long jet black hair hanging to her ass and a nice perfect tan complexion. Andy had to do something to get her attention so he did the first thing that came to his mind.

As he Rolls Royce pulled into the lot, Andy jumped in front of her half of a million dollar car. She hit the brakes.

"Get the fuck out the way before I hit you, crazy!" she yelled in her ghetto Spanish accent

Andy didn't move at all. He looked her in her bright green eyes, holding his ground, seeing he was pissing her off.

"Are you fucking high, asshole? Get out the road or I'ma hit you!" she screamed at him. She couldn't go around him because there were cars bunched in all around her.

Andy laid down on the ground in his Givenchy sweatsuit, going extra hard, and it was working. She got out of the car and walked up to him with a can of mace, pointing it at him.

"Get out my way," she said, standing over him

"Not until you give me your number and name."

"What? Are you serious? What type of thirsty shit is that?" she said with one hand on her thick hips.

"Look, ma, when I saw you over there, you did something to me and I wasn't going to let you leave here without letting you know that I want and need you," he said, seeing her finally smile showing her white Colgate teeth.

"You lucky I won't spray you." She laughed. "Get up so I can give you my number, boy. You got people out here staring at us like we crazy," she said, blushing non-stop.

They talked for a couple of seconds and exchanged numbers. She told him her name was Mia, that she was from the Bronx and she owned a nail and hair salon near Castle Hill projects. Andy bagged her and left the lot in his new car blasting a Chris Brown and Drake song.

Chapter 10

Newburgh, NY

Rell had just dropped off ten keys to his little cousin, who had a trap spot on Main Street. Last week, CB blessed him with 50 keys on the arm. Rell was amazed. He had never seen so many bricks in his life. He thought CB robbed a plug or something, but that wasn't the case because CB told him he had a constant plug. Rell had twenty keys left he was sitting on. Luckily he knew a lot of niggas selling weight so when he put a good price on the keys, they were moving like hotcakes! The product was so good fiends were overdosing on coke.

Rell was on his way to Middletown, which was twenty minutes away, to sell the rest of his keys to cap on his homie he knew for years.

Rell called Orianna on his car speaker only to get her voicemail. He knew she was at work, but he was calling to tell her to quit her job because he was about to come up so she never had to work again.

***

Mount Vernon, NY

Andy pushed the gas pedal on his Aston Martin through the streets of Mount Vernon, on his way to meet with his man Fire, who was a Jamaican.

The past couple of days he had been so focused on trying to find out who this Mad Max character was that he had been sidetracked on meeting his plug, who was in New York.

Wolf told him they may have bigger problems than the Jamaicans soon. Andy had no clue what he was talking about, but he was war ready.

Andy had been dealing with two women at once Mia - and Maryanna - but only conversation on the phone and Facetime. He was feeling both women. They had their shit together and they were dime pieces.

He pulled into the projects on 7th and 3rd into the back parking lot to see Fire in the playground area with two kids playing on the slide.

Andy and Fire had known each other since preschool. They always kept in touch and looked out for each other. So when Andy called him, he was more than willing to meet with him.

"Yooo, what's good?" Andy said, putting on his fake Jamaican accent

"Everythin' crisp," Fire replied, embracing Andy with his long dreads swinging down his back.

"That's all you, bro?" Andy asked, pointing at the two little girls playing on the playground.

"Yeah. I been putting in work," Fire said, smiling, looking at his daughters, whom he loved with a passion.

"I need some info. I ain't want to go in too deep on the phone, feel me?"

"Facts," Fire said, walking around in the playground area

"You know a nigga named Mad Max?"

When Andy said the name, Fire stopped as if a snake was in front of him.

"Mad Max is the real thing, mon, trus' me. The muthafucka crazy. He runs the Shower Posse in the State while his family runs the crew in Jamaica. Bro, these niggas ain't playing. They control a big drug ring in the Bronx and Brooklyn out here also," Fire said, now walking into the parking lot, leaving his kids unattended like most people did in the pj's.

"Damn. Where can I find him?"

"That's hard. He be underground a lot since his brother Zion died," Fire said.

"He's going to be a problem, I see," Andy said, turning around to see an ice cream truck down the street surrounded by kids and parents. When Andy turned back around, he saw a gun pointed at his face

"I'm sorry, Andy, but I need that two million dollars. I got kids, and somebody going to get that money, so why not me? I used to work for Zion. He was a good Rasta. You fucked up when you killed him, brother, but Mad Max going to kill everything you love. That's how he get down."

"Nigga, shut the fuck up and kill me, please."

Bloc! Bloc! Bloc! Bloc! Bloc!

Blood squirted on Andy's face as Fire's head busted open like a zit on a nigga face. Andy saw Demon stare at him and walk off.

Andy ran to his car, getting the fuck outta sight. He couldn't believe he almost let Fire do him dirty. Demon and him never had any words because the young boy didn't talk to anybody except Force, which was odd, but Andy made a future mental note to thank him.

***

Downtown Brooklyn

Mr. Cox was a Jewish lawyer with twenty-four years in the system. He had six more months before he could retire and move his family to Miami to enjoy his happy life. Mr. Cox had taken on some of the biggest cases to ever come out of Brooklyn. Some he lost, but most he won. He had his own law firm full of lawyers and thirsty rookies fresh out of college trying to make a name for themselves.

It was 6 p.m. and he was on his way home. Normally he was the first in the office and the last to leave. He heard someone come through the front door since the door beeped every time someone opened it.

"Excuse me, we are closed. Come back in the——" Mr. Cox's words were cut short when he saw the sexy Spanish woman in the mini dress and open blouse showing a little breast. "How can I help you?" Mr. Cox asked, checking his watch, seeing he had a couple of minutes to spare.

"You're Mr. Cox?" Maryanna asked.

"Yes, I am. And you are?"

"I have a message for you," Maryanna stated, going into her Fendi purse to pull out a gun.

Boc! Boc! Boc! Boc! Boc! Boc!

Maryanna saw his body backpedal into the desk, where he fell to die.

Chapter 11

Brooklyn, NY

"Ummm, shit, papi, yessss!" Karol screamed, feeling her husband's massive dick bang her guts out in missionary position.

Mad Max was putting in work, sweating as went deeper in Karol's moist pussy. "Whose pussy is this?"

"Yours, daddy. Ugghhh!"

"Louder," Mad Max said, shoving every inch inside her, making his balls clap the bottom of her ass.

"YOURS!" she yelled, unable to take all of it.

He picked up the pace, going deeper, pounding her phat pussy out until they both climaxed for the fourth time that night.

"Let's go take a shower, babe," Mad Max said, lifting her up and placing her in her wheelchair.

Karol was paralyzed from the waist down from a car accident she was in as a kid in Mexico. She was Jimenez's daughter, which nobody knew about because he kept her a secret for her own safety. She was beautiful with colorful eyes, long blonde hair, a phat ass, big breasts, nice smile, light skin, and a killer smile. When she posted a selfie, social media would go crazy. She was considered an Instagram model, but nobody ever saw her lower body; only her upper body. Mad Max had to marry her because her sex was still amazing and she was his ride or die since day one.

A group of biomedical engineers was working on a design for artificial limbs for her to use as legs so she could get around instead of having to use the wheelchair. Karol was the only thing he ever loved besides the two daughters they had.

They got in the warm handicapped shower and Karol sucked his dick for over thirty minutes. Her head game was crazy. She had no gag reflex and she would go crazy on the dick with her tongue ring.

***

Cross County, Yonkers

Wolf walked into his apartment after picking up some money Andy owed him. Wolf smelled the strong scent of perfume, which made him pull out the 9mm Beretta from his lower back. He creeped around the living room area, then made his way to the master bedroom, and when he saw a woman's backside in lingerie, all types of nasty thoughts filled his head. Her ass was hanging out of the lingerie and the panty line was stuck in her ass, which swallowed the whole thing.

"You can put the gun down. As you see, I come in peace," Salma said, looking at herself in the mirror.

"Can you at least put on some clothes?"

"You scared of a real woman?" she replied, seeing him walk into his walk-in closet to come out with a long Louis Vuitton T-shirt.

Wolf took one more glance at her body and tried hard to control himself while looking at her shaved pussy lips hanging out of her panties and her flat abs.

She put the shirt on and sat on his bed with her legs crossed in her heels, looking like a diva, staring at him with lust in her eyes. She knew it was wrong to want to fuck her lover's son, but she couldn't help it.

"I'm not even going to ask you how you got in here. What do you want?" Wolf asked, sitting in a chair near his fireplace, looking at her sexy legs.

"Last time we talked, I didn't tell you the whole truth and I left out so important information that you may need to know."

"So you come in here in lingerie to seduce me?"

"It's only seducing if you let the thought control your mind, so I call it temptation," Salma said.

"Get to the point."

"Some people are looking for you, and I believe it to be your wife. I heard this through the grapevine," Salma stated.

"Tell me something new."

"Oh, so you know? Well, that's not all. There is something I have to tell you about me. My name is Salma Aguilera," she said, now getting his full attention.

"So what, you come to kill me for your brother's grimy ways that led to his death?"

"No! At least, not yet."

"How about not ever?"

"Don't push it, papi. I knew what he was doing when he took the job given by your mother. You see, Ryan told me all about her, but he didn't know she was the one who wanted the both of you dead. But I did."

"So why didn't you say shit if you loved him?"

"Because that would have started a war I did not need at the time and I don't pillow talk."

"Why are you here now? For revenge?"

"I feel like it's my fault your father is dead. Because I didn't warn him," she stated sadly with her head down.

"A little too late, don't you think?" he added.

"Never too late, because I know who did it Wolf, your wife killed Ryan and I'm out for blood, so you can help or get in the way to be Mr. Save-a-Hoe and get crushed."

"I work alone. And make that the last time you threaten me," he said seriously.

"Or what?" she added, looking into his eyes, getting horny by his tough guy demeanor.

"I think it's time you leave," he said, grabbing her pea coat off the floor and handing it to her.

"I'll go. Do you really think my niece is coming back?" he laughed.

"I don't give a fuck about Bella."

"The feeling most be mutual because when you find out who she's fucking, your little heart is going to be crushed," Salma said, leaving, swaying her hips.

Wolf stared, trying to make sense out of what she was trying to say.

Romell Tukes

Chapter 12

Westchester County, NY

Rita had a nice 16, 546 square foot six bedroom and four and a half bathroom mansion in a nice gated upper class neighborhood. It was a glass house with two levels and marble white floors. The mansion had a majestic harbor front with a pool, floor to ceiling glass paneled windows, three spacious living areas which all opened to different balconies. Vernacular architecture baccarat chandeliers everywhere and Cambria granite countertops throughout the large kitchen.

Four personal security guards were hired just to watch over the house while she was home and they did just that.

Today was a perfect day to tan, so Rita was laying poolside, getting a tan in her bikini, showing off her toned sexy body and reading a magazine. Business was going well for her now that CB was home. She was using him as her go-to guy because she didn't trust a soul except family. Since Paola had taken over the Five Families operations, she had been dealing with her and she was about her business. She reminded Rita so much of Ruiz back in the day, only in a female body.

There was only one problem in her life and that was the issue she had been trying to take care of for months. But he just wouldn't die. Rita first had her daughter killed for her own personal reasons, and then she tried to eliminate Wolf, but the plan she thought out backfired many times.

At the moment she had no clue where Wolf was, but if she knew her son like she thought she did, then he would be somewhere lurking, trying to figure out why she wanted him dead. She wanted his father dead for many other reasons because she hated him with a passion. When she tried to use him to murder his son, she thought Ryan would take it because he was a snake like that. She made plans to kill him after he killed Wolf, but instead, they teamed up to solve the puzzle, and there was no doubt in her mind that they had figured everything out.

Rita wasn't dumb. She had been in the game long enough to know you always had to keep a plan B and C, and right now she was on plan F.

"Mom, what's up?" CB said, walking outside eating an apple with his new thick Cuban chain hanging. When he saw his mom's perfect body in her bikini he shook his head and tossed her a towel, but he had to give it to her. She was killing 75% of the chicks he saw in the streets and on social media.

"Boy, this my body and my house. Maybe you shouldn't be looking at your mom that way anyway," she said, taking off her shades, looking at his dick print in his shorts and then smiling.

"It's my eyes."

"Don't let your eyes get you in something you can't handle."

He looked to see if she was serious because it was getting weird and hot. "I can handle anything."

"You can? I think you scared."

"I'm scared of nothing," he replied with force in his voice.

"Okay. Stand up then," she said, sitting up and licking her lips. When he stood up, his dick was so hard it was about to bust out of his shorts. "Nasty, nasty," she said, rubbing his dick with her manicured nails. She then did the unthinkable and pulled his dick out to see his eyes grow wide. She rubbed his dick across her face. "Mmmmmm… Let me see how you taste, big boy, since you can handle it," Rita said, wrapping her thick lips around the tip, sucking it and then deep throating the whole dick while she twisted her neck, bopping her head up and down with no remorse.

"Ohhhh shittt," CB moaned, feeling weak in his knees. He never had no head like this. He grabbed her head and started to face fuck her and she let him. CB was so caught up in the moment he forgot it was his mother down there. She worked his dick in and out of her mouth like a Hoover vacuum on top speed. "I'm cummingggggg!" he screamed.

"Cum in my mouth," she said, deep throating him while holding herself there until she felt a big load shoot down the back of her throat. "Mmmmm," she moaned deeply, then looked him in his eyes to see his zombie.

CB fixed himself up before he fell over on the ground, almost falling in the pool, making her laugh because that was only a little tease.

"Get yourself together, son. We have to take care of your brother soon before he becomes an issue and we don't need any problems. First handle his friend Andy, because I believe he is the muscle, be smart," Rita said, not waiting for a reply, putting her face back into her magazine.

CB took off, breathing hard, shocked at what just went down. He had been peeping the way she had been eyeing him lately, but he never thought anything of it. He felt so wrong, but it felt so good. He wanted to turn around and go beat her back because he saw her in some thongs the other day and she had the prettiest little pussy that made a nigga want to suck on it.

But CB had to focus on Andy. He'd deal with his weird desires on another day, he thought to himself, leaving her crib, passing the guards in the front who all shook their heads because she had sucked all of them off once upon a time when she was horny.

Romell Tukes

Chapter 13

Park Chester, Bronx

Wolf had just come from looking at a rental space to open up a bookstore. It was a high traffic area and there wasn't even a Barnes and Noble around. There was a college nearby and students had nowhere close to purchase books, so Wolf knew a bookstore with all types of different books would attract students.

Looking in his rearview mirror, he saw a GMC truck tailing him. Wolf laughed as he pulled the BMW up to the light. Like clockwork, Wolf hopped out with a fully-loaded Draco and went to work

Tat-tat-tat-tat-tat-tat-tat-tat!

Wolf hit the driver twice in his chest and he shot the passenger in the head. Other cars pulled out, racing the opposite way to get away from the gunfire.

Tat-tat-tat-tat-tat-tat!

Bloc! Bloc! Bloc!

A gunman hopped out with a pistol, firing rounds at Wolf, but missing his target and shooting out the BMW's tail lights. Wolf took cover, looking around to see people on their phones who were most likely calling the police. Wolf hopped up, taking four shots at the gunman who was looking for him and hitting him with four bullets to the neck. When the last gunman hit the pavement, Wolf ran up to the car since he could hear sirens from a distance of at least five blocks away.

Wolf looked in the backseat, about to fire, but when he saw Paola's fearless face, he hesitated.

"Kill me now, Romeo, because this will be your only chance," Paola said calmly, but she was really scared after seeing him murder three of her best shooters.

Paola had gotten the drop on Wolf days ago and today she was going to put him to rest. She told the driver to keep a good distance, but he would not listen.

Wolf couldn't even reply. He just ran off, hopping in his BMW, and raced off on the exit leading to the FDR parkway.

***

Westchester, NY

Trigger was in Rye at the Playland amusement park, walking around. The place was jammed this weekend with kids and civilians having fun with their families. Trigger had come here alone to meet his connect at the Zombie roller coaster entrance.

Trigger met his plug when he was in Miami at a club called G5. He thought his plug was a bartender and dancer when she plugged up to him. That night he tricked off over 70K in two hours and his plug watched him closely that whole night. Trigger was chilling in his VIP section that night and she had just come and sat down next to him, asking him if he was from Yonkers, NY because he looked familiar. When he told her that he was, it sparked up a conversation, and one thing led to another. She asked him what he did for a living and he was honest. She offered to help him, and ever since that day, Rita had been supplying him. Trigger knew she was Black's and CB's mom. He knew of Wolf by name, but had never met him.

He saw Rita sitting on the green wood bench, watching the roller coaster go through the tunnel, eating cotton candy. Trigger couldn't deny how sexy she was looking in her short white Chanel dress and high heels.

"Hey beautiful," Trigger said, approaching her as she stood up to give him a hug. When he saw her curves, he bit his lip because she was bad and her body was on point.

"Thanks for coming. Cotton candy?" she said, handing him a stick she bought for him.

"Sure. You look sexy, ma. I can't front. You make a nigga wanna suck the crust off your feet," Trigger said making her blush harder than ever before.

"Please, Trigger, you wouldn't know what to do with me, boy."

"Let me show you," he said, taking her hand and rubbing it against his dick.

"Ummm, okay, but just because you have a big dick don't mean you know how to use it?" she quizzed him.

"Find out."

"Maybe one day I will. But let's walk and take care of business," she said, walking through the crowds of people.

"I got the money in section four parked in a blue Dodge Neon," Trigger said, getting straight to the point.

"Perfect. I will have my man follow you in a van with your order in it. Wherever you want it, they will deliver it to you. I believe it's best we handle business transactions like this from here on out because this is going to be a hot summer, and I don't need unwanted attention."

"I'm cool with that. Just give me a time and a place."

"I will. But off topic…do you know a kid named Andy from Elm Street?" Rita asked, passing the food court.

"Yeah. He used to live in the same building as me and my little brother Lil Tom, may he rest in peace."

"Do you have any info on him?"

"Not really. From what I hear, he lost everything he loved last year in a war with the Mexicans and the Crips," Trigger said, trying to figure out her agenda because Andy was his main client. But he wasn't going to tell her that. Trigger was focused on chasing a bag; not beef.

"Okay. Just asking. I have to go. I'll be in touch. And I'ma take you up on your offer one day. Just don't be scared when I throw this big ass back on that dick," she said, walking off.

Romell Tukes

Chapter 14

White Plains, NY

"Let me get a number four, and no pickles or mayo please," Spice asked the clerk behind the Wendy's counter who took his order with an attitude like it was his fault she was working at a fast food joint. Spice shook his head and turned around, bumping into a beautiful Spanish woman with the craziest set of eyes he had ever seen in his life. He could tell she was Mexican. She looked like she could be a model.

"Excuse me, beautiful. I'm sorry," Spice said, looking at her manicured painted toes in her flip flops.

"It's cool, papi," Julie said, smiling, thinking he was cute, but nothing past that. Julie ordered her salad and sat at a table next to Spice, who was peeking at her, but when she looked at him, he would focus his attention on something else. "Since you too scared to say something...hey, I'm Julie," she said, seeing the surprised look on his face.

"You talking to me?" Spice asked, trying to play it cool, but he was really shaking in his boots.

"No, I'm talking to the person behind you! Yes, I'm talking to you," Julie added, trying to hold back her laughs.

"I'm Spice from Newburgh. I can't lie, you bad, ma, but you seem like the bougie type."

"Never, papi. I'm a Cali girl from the poverty of Honduras. I just carry myself with class and respect," she said before one of the employees called both of them to get their food.

"I guess you never judge a book by its cover."

"True."

"So what are you doing in New York?" Spice asked the question she knew was coming.

"I'm here on business. I'm starting my own clothing line and I'm here to meet with some big name people," she said, walking out of the fast food restaurant with him.

"What's the name of your clothing line?"

"Huh?" she said as he caught her off-guard

"What's the name of your clothes so I can look out for them," Spice said, wondering if she was lying just to sound like she was on something.

"Ohhh. It's called Heartless." She said the first thing that came to mind.

"Catchy. I like that."

"I have to go. Thanks for the vibes."

"So a nigga can't get your number or social media?" Spice asked.

"Nope."

"I'll find you," Spice mumbled to himself when she pulled off, wondering how could she afford that Bentley with a clothing line not even off the ground. There was something about her he liked, so he memorized her license plate to do some research on her because he got a funny vibe from her.

***

San Quentin Prison, Cali
Days later

Ruiz had a visit, which was a surprise to him because nobody told him they were coming, but Ruiz appreciated all the support. He wore his Cartier frames and fresh jumper with a gold cross chain worth 1.2 million dollars.

The two guards opened the visit room doors for him since he was cuffed in shackles from waist, hands, to ankles. Ruiz was brought to a small booth with a stool and a phone. When Ruiz saw who was on the other side of the window, his smile turned into an evil frown. Ruiz sat down after he was uncuffed and picked up the phone.

"You grimy little bitch! After all I did for you!" Ruiz shouted

"Ruiz, it's not like that. The way the shit went down wasn't part of the plan. I'm sorry," Rita stated seriously.

"You got my brother buried and you come up here with an apology? All these years we been dealing with each other you never crossed me or any member of the Five Families."

"That wasn't my intention," Rita told him, trying to justify what Ryan and Wolf did to his people.

"You set that shit up, Rita. I know you, mami. You're too smart to make a move and not know the outcome to your actions. I should have never agreed to put my people in your mix, and now look. They all dead," Ruiz said, slamming his fist into the steel table.

"I'ma leave now, Ruiz. I had just come to apologize for the loss of your brother and people, but I won't let you disrespect me," Rita said, pushing her seat back, ready to leave.

"Rita, you crossed the line and used me. I will make sure you pay for what you have done to my family," Ruiz told her.

"Is that a threat, Ruiz? Because if it is, I will kill everything you love," she replied, staring in his cold evil eyes.

"I don't make threats, and you know this better than anyone. I forgive you for what you have done because now my children can take over what I build. All I'm saying is to never bite the hand that feeds you." Ruiz looked at her, not blinking an eye.

"I feed myself, Ruiz. Without me, your little empire or operation wouldn't be shit. Have a good time doing a thousand burpees," Rita said, leaving.

Ruiz knew she was right. Rita had given Ruiz a couple of million to start his empire from scratch after he fucked up a lot of coke and he was robbed by the Cubans. That had left him at ground zero until Rita came along.

Romell Tukes

Chapter 15

Yonkers, NY

Force was driving his Hellcat past The Hole, which was a projects known for its deadly violence and crime wave, especially in the summer. Force had just come from a night basketball game near his own hood. Force was one of the best ballplayers in the city. He knew if he hadn't chosen the streets, then he would have been in the NBA making millions.

He had been so busy dealing with the Jamaicans and trying to find a location on Mad Max that he was unable to make time for his personal life. His mom recently found out she had been diagnosed with cancer and he hadn't had the time to go check on her. His mom used to be a crackhead until she got her life together and started doing NA meetings to help other addicts get clean and get their life in order.

Once he was a block away, he stopped at a red light to see construction workers out fixing the roads. But all they were doing was sweeping and placing orange cones everywhere. Force found it odd that the construction workers all had dreads and weren't doing any type of construction work in his plain view.

***

Audrey stopped at a red light to see construction workers standing around doing nothing except cleaning the street.

She had been in Yonkers for a couple of days now. She stayed in a nice fancy hotel and drove a Lexus coupe. She was in Yonkers on a mission and she wasn't leaving until it was complete.

Audrey saw one of the construction workers pull out an AK-47 assault rifle, and that's when the street turned into Iraq.

The Jamaicans all pulled out assault rifles, spraying rounds at the Hellcat across from her, but the driver was already out of his car with a Draco in hand as if he saw it coming. Watching the twelve gunmen fire a round towards the young, tall, handsome kid, she knew he had no chance. The kid had hit three of the shooters already, then two more. She was surprised.

She couldn't just sit there and watch them take him, plus she thought he was kinda cute and she hated Jamaicans. Audrey popped out with an AR-15 assault rifle with a laser.

Tat-tat-tat-tat-tat!

She took out five of the shooters with perfect headshots and the young guy took out the other two as they tried to run from the AR-15 bullets Audrey was firing like a mad woman.

"Shit!" Force said, seeing his tires were shot out along with his windows. He saw the woman who saved his life pull up in a Lexus.

"Come on!" she said, opening the passenger door from inside the car.

Force jumped in with no other choice, hoping it wasn't a set-up.

When they got away from the crime scene, Force looked at her up close for the first time and she was a work of art. He could tell she was Spanish because of her features. Her skin was a nice tan. She had curly long hair, hazel eyes, dimples, a nose ring, and long eyelashes. Force couldn't lie. She was every man's dream. But he was confused because she came out of nowhere.

"Thank you."

"No problem. I could tell you needed a little help back there," she said with her eyes focused on the road.

"Somewhat. But where did you learn to shoot like that?"

"I was in the Navy SEALs. You ask a lot of questions. The question should be, why was them people shooting at you?" she asked, now looking at him with a smirk.

"You hungry?"

"Nice change of subject," she said as he directed her to a nice restaurant, where they spend hours getting to know each other.

***

Auburn Maximum Security Prison

OG Chuck had just gotten a letter in the mail call from CB, which made him smile, but he still regretted not having the balls to tell him he was his father. Once in his cell, he opened the letter and sat down to read it.

"OG, what's poppin'? I'm just sending my love and regards. How you holding up in there? I just sent you a couple of stacks and a 35 pound food package with the shit you like. I'ma try to do that once a month, even though I know you good. Life is looking bright. I'm focused and on the grind. I'm doing everything I said I would. Holla back. Love-n-respect always..."

OG put the letter down and grabbed his paper and pen to write back.

***

L. A., Cali

Rita was putting on the last touches of her makeup before she left the hotel to catch her flight back to New York. She brought three guards with her and they were all waiting down stairs for her.

The visit with Ruiz didn't go as planned, but Rita couldn't care less. She was focused on her business. One thing she learned early in the game was not to let someone else's feelings or emotions control you or your business plans.

Rita left her room with her big Birkin bag on her shoulder, heading downstairs.

"Good morning, boss lady," one of her guards said, waiting in the lobby.

"You know I'm not a morning bitch. Let's just get out of here," she said, walking through the sliding doors and out of the lobby.

Before she got to the rental truck, she realized she forgot her phone. "Damn, I forgot my phone. I'll be back," Rita said, turning around, making her way back upstairs while the guards got in the Tahoe SUV.

Boom!

Rita heard the loud explosion and turned to see the Tahoe blown into pieces and on fire, killing her men. People ran outside, thinking it was a terrorist attack.

Chapter 16

Manhattan, NY

Lance stepped outside his condo in a clean all-black Tom Ford suit, smoking a big cigar, looking at himself in the window of his Ferrari limousine. Lance was a tycoon. He owned businesses, sold real estate, and sold drugs to other mob families in New York, New Jersey, and Boston. His father was an honorable Mobster from Brooklyn before he died in federal prison from a heart attack. Lance was one of the most trustworthy mobsters left in the city, so he carried his name with honor and respect.

Lance hopped in his limo for his 1 p.m. appointment in Queens with another Mafia family to talk about opening a new restaurant and a couple of whore houses in Queens and Long Island. His goons were already awaiting his arrival in Queens. He didn't like to travel with an army unless it was called for. The limo driver made a turn towards a shopping center parking lot.

"What the fuck are you doing?" Lance yelled once the car came to a stop. "Heyyy asshole!" Lance yelled until he heard the loud gunfire in the front area. Lance was spooked when he heard the front door open and close. He saw a Spanish-looking kid walking towards him with a gun at his side. Lance got up, crawling to lock the door, but Wolf snatched it open just in the nick of time.

"In a rush?" Wolf asked, climbing in the backseat, pointing his gun at Lance, who was now shaking uncontrollably.

"Who the fuck are you? This has to be a mistake. I've done nothing wrong to nobody."

"I'm Rita's son and from my understanding, you're a client of hers?" Wolf asked.

"So? Business is business. I have nothing to do with her personal affairs!" Lance cried out

"I see things a little different, Lance. Maybe that's because I have an old soul. But ask yourself this: when it comes to blood, money is your blood. Is it more valuable than the people who shed their blood to get it?"

Before he could reply, Wolf shot him in the face ten times then called an Uber while walking into a Chinese store to order some egg rolls and a Pepsi.

***

Yonkers, NY

Thirty minutes later, Wolf was in the Uber, looking out the window, trying to put some plans together. As the Uber drove past some restaurants and bars, Wolf saw two familiar faces, but he had to do a double take when the Uber stopped at a red light on the busy street.

Wolf was stuck when he saw CB and Bella out having lunch, laughing and smiling outside of a steakhouse restaurant. Bella looked so beautiful. He felt jealousy and rage overcome his body. He couldn't believe his ex and his brother were an item. The Uber pulled off and Wolf was turning in his seat, staring at them.

***

Brooklyn, NY
Weeks later

Force rode in Demon's Camaro in silence, thinking about Audrey. The two had been together since the first day they met. Audrey ended up moving in with him yesterday and they had finally made love. He was hooked. She had the best pussy he ever had.

"What's up, bro? Why you so quiet?" Force asked Demon, who was speeding through the streets of Brooklyn, on his way to a Caribbean restaurant where Mad Max spent a lot of time at. Force had paid a nigga $10,000 in cash to find out where Mad Max chilled at and a young nigga from the Flatbush section reached out to Force with some info because Mad Max had killed his father last year.

"I'm cool, you heard, boy? Just ready to shed some blood," Demon said.

"I know the feeling. But you been on your meds lately?" Force asked, knowing how serious his friend's mental health problem could be at times.

"Yeah, why you ask?" Demon got on the defense side because Demon hadn't taken his medicine in a month. Demon used to have trouble with depression, angry, anxiety, suicide, and hearing voices. He still suffered from all these issues, but he tried to conceal them. Force would catch him talking to himself at times and when he asked Demon who he was talking to, he would say his demons.

"Just checking, bro. Don't kill me."

"You need to mind your business," Demon said seriously, pulling up across the street from the small yellow restaurant, which had two black SUVs parked in the front.

"A'ight, homie," Force said, not the one for arguing or going back and forth.

"That's them coming out," Demon said, grabbing his M4 off the backseat and handing Force his SK with a knife attached to the barrel.

***

Mad Max walked out of his restaurant to take care of some business with one of his clients across town. When he looked across the street, he saw two young niggas coming his way with big assault rifles. Before he could holler, shots were fired and one of his goons was hit

Tat-tat-tat-tat-tat-tat-tat-tat-tat!

Mad Max took cover and fired back five shots, almost hitting Demon.

Boc! Boc! Boc! Boc! Boc!

Force hit two more of Mad Max's goons in the vicious gun battle in the middle of the street.

Tat-tat-tat-tat-tat-tat-tat-tat!

Mad Max hit the ground behind the SUV, seeing his goons drop next to him. He was the last man left, so he fired seven shots at the gunmen and crawled back into the restaurant, where he had a safe room.

Force and Demon saw him go inside and they shot out the windows of the restaurant, about to go inside until they heard sirens. They looked at each other and ran to the Camaro, getting ghost before the police and coroner arrived.

Chapter 17

Manhattan, NY
Days later

It was a couple of minutes before 11 p.m. when Wolf walked into the five star fancy hotel with a shiny lobby marble floor and expensive paintings throughout the halls. Wolf had received a call from Salma earlier asking him to meet her here so they could talk. Wolf wanted to know how she got his number, but he didn't even bother to ask because he was starting to see she had her own way of doing shit.

The last couple of days he couldn't get the thought out of his head about Bella and CB. He wondered if they were sexually involved.

He got off the elevator at the penthouse floor to see double doors open down the hall. Walking down the hall, he heard an Avant album playing from inside the suite. Once inside, he saw the light was dim and candles were burning. Wolf shook his head, about to turn and leave, until he saw Salma come out of the kitchen in a silk robe and heels. She had her hair down to her hips. She looked better than last time. Her skin was glowing and her blue eyes were sparkling.

"What's this about?" Wolf said, walking into the living room, which was large, colorful, and had a state of the art surround sound system.

"I called you so we can talk. Take one," she said, passing him a small container filled with a green slushy drink.

"What's this?"

"A Finding Nemo. It's from the Heights. Just drink it," she replied, drinking hers with a thick straw as she sat down.

"You ain't poison this, did you?" he asked with a serious look, making her laugh.

"No. If I wanted you dead, I would have done it. I know where you live in Cross County and I know your every move," she said, letting him know she was on to him.

"Am I supposed to be impressed? I need a drink anyway," Wolf said, tasting the cold drink mixed with liquor and molly and ecstasy.

"I want to speak to you about us teaming up. I know you work alone, but soon you will have so many people coming for your head that you won't know who is who."

"So I'm supposed to trust you?"

"Well, I'm all you got. Wolf, how long you think it's going to be before the Jamaicans kill your friend Andy and his little crew? You need someone with an army who will have your back," she said, uncrossing her legs so he could get a closer look at her bald pussy under her robe because she wore no underclothes.

"What's in it for you?"

"I see you're smart enough to know the third rule in business, which is that there is always an agenda. I want to supply Yonkers. Your town is a gold mine. I want to eventually take over Westchester."

"Let me think about it and speak to my partner, because he currently has a plug." Wolf was referring to Andy.

"That's funny, Wolf, because your mother, who wants you dead, supplies Andy's plug Trigger, so when shit hits the fan - and it will soon - whose side will Trigger choose?" she asked.

Wolf had no clue his mom was Trigger's plug. He didn't know him, but Andy talked about him from time to time and this could be dangerous.

"I'll give you some time to think about it. So do you like the drink?" she asked, seeing it was starting to kick in.

"It was good, but I feel like I took a pill or something," Wolf said, licking his lips.

"That's a Finding Nemo, Wolf," she said, standing up. "Wolf, I been thinking and I want to suck your dick," she said, dropping her robe in front of him.

When he saw her thick thighs, flat stomach, and phat little pussy with her clit sticking out, his dick instantly got hard. Wolf couldn't say a word. All he did was unbuckle his Gucci belt while she got on her knees.

Salma pulled out his dick and wasted no time stuffing him in her mouth, slowly bopping her head up and down on his dick. She went slow and then fast while massaging his balls, slurping and giving him sloppy head. After ten minutes of sucking she realized he was never going to cum so she stopped.

"Damn, why you stop?" he asked, opening his eyes.

"Fuck me," she said, climbing on top of him so she could ride his masterpiece. She placed the tip in and worked her way down as he opened her tight pussy walls

"Mmmm…shit, you so wet," he said, feeling like he was in heaven.

"Yesss, fuck this pussy, papi!" she yelled, bouncing up and down on the dick, feeling her climax building.

Wolf grabbed her wide hips and started fucking her roughly as if he was angry, but it was turning her on by the second. When she came on his dick, Wolf bent her over and fucked her from the back, gripping on her phat soft ass until she cried out for him to stop because she couldn't take all the dick.

The two fucked for hours before crashing in the master bedroom on the floor.

***

Brooklyn, NY

"Thanks for coming, Ms. Rita. My father and mother speaks highly of you, but your son and his crew are becoming a big problem for me," Mad Max said, sitting in his H3 Hummer in a Family Dollar store lot with Rita in the backseat next to him. She was looking like a snack in a pink bodycon suit showing her nice breasts and phat camel toe.

"Kill him," Rita stated.

"Huh?" Mad Max asked, thinking he heard wrong.

"Kill him. I'm sure you have enough goons."

"I do. I just wanted your blessing because I did some research and found out you were his mother."

"Handle your business. Tell your parents I said hi," she said before climbing out of the truck to sway her hips back to her lambo.

Mad Max looked at her ass, wishing he could tap that. He knew how powerful she was so he didn't want to create a bigger war than he already had.

Chapter 18

Yonkers, NY

"That's crazy how you ran outta all that shit so fast, bro," CB said, driving through the dark streets of Yonkers on his way to North Blvd to his stash house.

"Bro, that work is fire and niggas is loving it. I can't even imagine how much money I missed in the last twenty-four hours," Rell said in the passenger seat of the Porsche Macan GTS that CB had recently bought to trap in.

"This shit going to make us rich, bro. I told you when I was up north we gonna take the game over, son," CB said, pulling up in front of a row of brick buildings.

"Facts, bro. But I'm about to have a seed, bro. Orianna pregnant"

"Damn, bro, how many kids you already got?" CB said, getting out of the car.

"Nigga, you got a lot of jokes, but——"

Boc! Boc! Boc! Boc! Boc! Boc! Boc! Boc! Boc!

Rell caught two bullets to the head and two to the chest before his body hit the curb, breaking his fall.

CB was so in shock he couldn't move because he didn't see that coming at all. When bullets wove past his head, he got low and pulled out his pistol and fired back.

Bloc, Bloc, Bloc, Bloc, Bloc, Bloc!

The gunmen hit on the side of a corner store

"Let's play, nigga! You wanna play tough?" CB yelled, firing seven shots like a madman.

The gunman fired four shots back until his gun got jammed. Andy was pissed he had missed his chance, but he turned and ran to his Benz parked a few feet away and pulled off.

CB saw the Benz's tail lights as it busted a sharp right at the end of the block. CB had seen Andy's face so he already knew it was a hit, but he was glad he made it because he only had three shots left.

He saw Rell lying dead, bleeding from his head and chest on the pavement. There was nothing he could do and that was the hard part. CB climbed in the Porsche, making a U-turn, in tears because losing Rell was like losing a family member.

***

Westchester, NY

Rita was in her exercise room doing her morning workout at 7 a.m. Today was light weights and cardio for her. She wore leggings, a sports bra, and Nike Zoom track sneakers, sweating from head to toe. Later on she had a meeting in New Jersey to expand with some Italians she had known for years. The death of Lance almost sparked a drug war with the Mafia and Columbians. They thought it was a Columbian cartel boss who called the hit on Lance because of disagreements.

Mary J. Blige was playing on the stereo while she was doing arm curls with the fifteen pound dumbbells. Rita looked at her TV monitor, which showed footage around the mansion, and what she saw made her grab her AR-15 assault rifle from out of the closet. She saw a masked man killing her guards without even breaking a sweat upstairs. When she made it upstairs, she saw the gunman sitting at her dining room table with a M5 assault rifle.

"Why don't you show your face before I kill you?" Rita demanded, walking toward him, pointing her assault rifle at him in combat mode.

When the mask came off, she put her weapon down and looked at her son. "You could have just rang the doorbell like normal people," she told Wolf before sitting down at the dining room table, placing her AR-45 next to a plate.

"It was you the whole time. I can't believe it! My own mother," Wolf stated, feeling a little hurt now that he was face to face with her.

"You never understand, Romeo. You was the chosen one. Maryanna taught you well, but you will always be your father's son.

Since you were a kid you was just different and advanced, but I would have never been able to show you this way of life because you have a murderous mentality and people like you could never be trusted," Rita said.

"So you used me to kill Aguilera, his flunkies, and the Five Families, and let's not forget my pops."

"I had to use you some type of way. You have an amazing talent. What can I say?"

"You should have hired a hitman."

"I did. You killed him, remember? Mickey?"

"You sent him to kill me," Wolf said

"I was helping you better your craft, son."

"I bet."

"What are you here for, a bedtime story? You found out where I live. Good job."

"I just came to wish you a happy birthday!"

"Thank you. I'm happy you remembered. You're the only child who remembered."

"That's because you killed them all," Wolf said, standing up to leave.

"Maybe, but everyone has their day I'm sure yours will be soon"

"Hope not sooner than yours," Wolf replied, walking out of her home.

***

Flatbush, Brooklyn

Linda was Mad Max's little sister who went to college and worked a part time job to support herself because she didn't want anything from her drug dealing family. She was twenty-two, plus-sized, with a cute face, short hair, and a big ole ass most niggas couldn't handle.

Linda walked into her boyfriend's building. She lived with him in the hood surrounded by gangs, killings, shootings, sex trafficking, and drug dealers.

Opening the door, she was attacked by two men and one covered her mouth so she wouldn't scream. Linda bit his hand and he slapped her to the ground with the pistol.

"Chill, bro. Sit her up, son," Demon told his two young boys. He was grooming Phil and E Baby.

Linda spit out blood on the floor, but when she saw the puddle of blood near her hand, she looked to her left to see her boyfriend's dead body.

"Ohhh noooo! Please...oh my God!" she cried out loud, making Demon laugh.

"Where can we find Mad Max, ma. And please don't play no games," Demon asked, seeing she was remaining silent. Demon nodded his head at E Baby, who was fifteen years old and a vicious killer.

E Baby grabbed Linda, bent her over on the couch, and pulled up her skirt, ripping off her panties and ramming his dick in her big pussy. E Baby spread her ass cheeks and pounded her big ass out, making her moan in pleasure and fear.

Damn, that shit stank! Phil covered his nose.

E Baby was going as deep as he could inside that fishy twat. Once he nutted in her, Linda looked at him like she wasn't impressed.

"He got a couple of spots and he normally be at a poker house on London Avenue or the one on Fulton Avenue," she said before Demon fired three rounds into her head.

Chapter 19

Yonkers, NY

Trigger saw the white Aston Martin pull up behind him and he turned off the engine so he could talk to Andy, his client and friend. The two went way back. They were always close and when Lil Tom was killed, they got a little closer. Today Trigger would see where their friendship really stood.

"Yoooo, what's goody, son?" Andy said, hopping in the passenger seat and embracing Trigger because this was the first time he saw him face to face since Lil Tom's funeral.

"Ain't shit, bro. I'm up here for a while. The A was getting a little hot, feel me?" Trigger asked, looking at Andy, who was checking his surroundings outside.

"I feel you, fam, but I'm ready for you, bro. Shit is desert dry. My people be running through all that shit, son." Andy saw twenty motorcycles race by doing tricks with Ruff Ryder logos on their jackets and bikes.

"Before we handle business affairs I need to speak to you because something has popped up and before we can continue our business arrangements, I need to know where you stand."

"As far as what?"

"You know a kid named Wolf from Elm Street?"

"Yeah, why, what's shaking?" Andy asked, keeping his hand close to his right thigh just in case he had to get to his weapon on his hip.

"Let's say a very important person wants him dead and is offering a lot of money to have his head along with a lot of keys that would set you straight for life," Trigger stated, seeing Andy listen in deep thought.

"Okay, let me make one thing clear. I'm loyal to those loyal to me. No money or drugs will ever change that, fam. Facts," Andy said as Trigger nodded his head.

"So you do know where this leaves us right?"

"Do you? Because it looks like you're on the wrong side," Andy said before getting out to go meet Mia for their little date in the Bronx at a pool hall on Gunhill Road.

***

Bronx, NY
Hours later

"Four ball, left pocket," Mia said, bending over the pool table in her tight jeans, showing her curves which was a gift from God.

Mia had finally agreed to meet with Andy at a pool hall to play pool and have some drinks. She was a simple girl because she already had everything anybody could ask for.

"Ten ball, left corner," Andy said, shooting the ball down the table, but missing his shot.

"Let me find out you missing on purpose, Andy," she said, showing her sexy smile before taking a sip of Henny.

"Maybe anything to keep you playing," he said, seeing her shoot the 8 ball in the hole, winning the game four times in a row.

"You lucky I don't gamble, papi, because if I did, you'd be leaving here on an EBT card," she said, making him laugh.

Andy liked her personality. She was different, but she had a thug side to her that he loved. He was dealing with Mia and Maryanna at the same time, and they both were playing hard to get.

"I see you wearing that off-white," Andy said, checking out her outfit and ladies Rolex.

"Somethin' light, papi," she replied.

"Question. What do you do for a living? Because I never saw a female whip a Rolls Royce fresh off the lot paid for."

"How do you know it's paid for?"

"Because I asked the salesman," Andy said, making her look at him like he was a stalker.

"Damn, what type of shit you on?" she said, laughing but serious.

"I just wanted to know about you."

"You could have asked, nosy. My ex-boyfriend recently went to the feds and he left me a lot of drugs and money. His people took the drugs," she stated.

"Okay, I see."

"Yeah, I already had two salons and nail parlors. Now I want to open a Latina restaurant in Spanish Harlem or on Broadway," she said, telling him her goals.

She liked Andy because he was a good listener and she could tell he had his shit in order, unlike most niggas who was looking for a come up off a woman.

"That's what's up. You're on the grind."

"Facts," Mia stated, ordering another round of drinks for them. They kicked it for another hour, then made plans for the weekend.

***

South Central, Cali

Mario was normally the first person at the moving company in the mornings. Today was a big day because a shipment of dope and coke was arriving at 12 p.m.

Mario walked through the loading dock area to his office to make some calls. He had a hangover because last night he was in a big Hollywood party and he left with four bitches who wanted to have fun all night. He was up late sniffing coke and drinking. With only two hours of sleep, he knew an energy drink was well needed.

Stepping into his office, he turned on the light to see a sexy Spanish bitch sitting on his desk top in a short dress and heels with a big Glock in her hand.

"What's going on? Who are you?"

"I'm a friend, and I come to claim what's mine, Mario. I put in blood, sweat, and tears to one day take over the Five Families operations, and here you are," Julie said, standing up.

"You can have it all, please. Just let me go," Mario said moving his hand to his lower back where his gun was.

Julie shot him in his hand.

"Ahhhhh!"

"I'm going to take everything I deserve and eliminate anybody in the way," she said before shooting him twice in his heart, then six times in the face.

She walked out to see two men walking towards her and she shot them both, killing them on her way out.

Chapter 20

Jersey Shore Beach, NJ

It was a nice warm sunny day on the beach and everybody was out going for a swim or catching a tan.

"You got a nice body," Audrey said, lying on a beach towel, looking like a Victoria Secret model with her bikini hugging her perfect frame.

"You do too. I'm trying to see how you taste?" Forces said, relaxing next to her shirtless, showing the chiseled body women loved.

"I don't think you're ready for me."

"That's what your mouth says. But anyway, tell me, what's your goals and plans in life?" he asked her playing in her long curly hair, looking into her bright hazel colored eyes.

"To be honest, I don't really know. I'm a day by day type chick. I may go back to the Navy or maybe make a family, but first I need to take care of some important family issues," she replied, being honest.

She had been kicking it with Force hard lately. The two thought they were soulmates, but what was crazy to them was how they were born the same year and had the same birthday.

Force let her crash at his condo instead of living in a hotel. He knew it would be cool to have a woman around the crib. He had three bedrooms so he gave her one and a bathroom so she could have privacy. Audrey was gone most of the time so he barely saw her but when he did, they would go shopping, out to eat, to beaches, clubs, amusement parks, just to loosen up and have a little fun.

"I understand."

"Where is your family? You seem so independent and private with your life and past. I be trying to figure you out, but you're too hard to figure out," she said, looking at a group of white boys walk past, looking at her long sexy legs and pussy print that could be seen from a mile away.

"I don't really have too much of a family, ma. My story is like every other nigga's in the hood, but I don't let my past bring me down or hold me back. I saw a lot at a young age and I lost a lot at a young age. Mama luv been on drugs my whole life, so I guess it's cool to say I'm a crack baby. My pops...I don't even want to speak of him. My little brother died when he was only three from the flu. My grandparents tried to raise me until they both died from cancer when I was ten years old." He stared into the clouds, thinking about his hardships growing up alone in the slums of Yonkers. There were times when his mom turned the apartment into a crack house and fiends were running in and out at all hours of the night on school nights so he couldn't sleep. He thought back to the times he didn't have lunch money to eat food at lunch, so he would rob other kids' food because he knew that would be his last meal of the day.

"I'm sorry to hear that. But at least you became a good person," she said looking at him,

They felt a strong connection that second, so they reached in for a kiss. The kiss was so deep and passionate that they felt a shock wave vibrate through their bodies.

"Damn," Force said, making her blush.

"How about we go eat? I'm starving," she said, grabbing his head, standing up and showing her perfect, ample ass.

***

Sleepy Hollow, NY

"Oh my God," Bella said, ass naked, climbing off CB's dick after riding over forty minutes straight. The sheets were extra wet, soaked in most areas. She had squirted twice. CB had never seen anything like it. Bella fucked CB so good she had him crying tears of joy.

They were chilling, eating, and watching TV, then one thing led to another and he was eating her out. After the oral sex, they started fucking like two wild animals.

"You're amazing, Isabella," CB said, admiring her beauty and thinking how she had the best pussy he ever had. CB knew she was the full package, but now that he knew her sex game was crazy, he was ready to take it to the next level.

"So are you, big daddy. You beat my little pussy out the box. I'm so sore. I know everybody in the building heard me yelling," she said, laughing.

"I gotta go meet my mom. I'll hit you later. We still on for dinner?" CB asked, getting dressed.

"Facts."

"When you going to introduce me to your mom?" she asked.

"Soon. I'm just waiting on the right time, baby."

"Oh, okay, good," Isabella said, ready to take a shower and clean up her room because semen and condom wrappers were everywhere. CB really put in that work. She was in love.

***

Westchester Community College, NY

Rachel walked through the financial aid building after waiting in line for over an hour to make sure her up and coming semester was fully paid. She was Demon's sister and the complete opposite of her brother. She was short, brown-skinned, a green-eyed blonde with long hair, a phat ass, and small titties a nigga could suck on while he was fucking her. Rachel was taking journalism classes to become a writer one day. That was her dream.

She had to take a piss. She had been holding it for over an hour, so she went to the nearest bathroom. Stepping in the restroom, she ran into the stall and wiped the toilet seat before taking a piss. When she was done, she opened the door to the stall to see a Jamaican man standing there with a knife. She was about to run when he stabbed her in her neck and then attacked her upper body, hitting her thirty-eight times and leaving her dead body by the toilet.

Romell Tukes

Chapter 21

Newburgh, NY
Days later

Spice and Julie spent the evening at the boardwalk at the riverfront where all the bars and restaurants were located. Two weeks ago Spice had received a friend request from Julie on his Facebook page. She was looking like a snack on social media. She had 80,000 friends and on her Instagram she had 4.4 million followers. She was litty.

"It's nice out here," Julie said, looking at all the boats lined up on the water.

"Yeah, I come out here sometime to get peace of mind because I be having so much shit going on. I be feeling lost at times," Spice stated, holding her hand as they walked side by side, enjoying the stars in the sky.

"It seems like you have a perfect life: big chain, nice watch, AP bust down shit, nice cars...how can you be lost?" she asked.

"Sometimes money can't buy happiness or love," Spice said, stopping and looking her in her eyes, which he always got lost in. "I've been thinking about you since I first laid eyes on you and I want you, Julie," Spice stated seriously, seeing she was at a loss for words.

"Wow," was all she could say.

"Wow what?"

"Just overwhelmed. I like you too. I just want to take it one day at a time," she told him.

"Okay, I'm with that. How's your clothing line?"

"My what?" Julie shot back, confused

"Your clothing line you said you had?" Spice was looking at her like she was a liar.

"Oh yeah, it's going good. I have another big meeting in Manhattan tomorrow so I do have to get back to the city soon," she said checking her watch looking at the diamonds encrusted in the face.

"Let me walk you to your car," Spice said, making plans for another date.

***

Spanish Harlem, NY

Andy was speeding through Spanish Harlem to meet Mia at a hair salon she owned. He had just left Maryanna twenty minutes ago in the Bronx. Both women had his nose wide open. He didn't know who he liked better because both women were special and dime pieces.

He stopped at a corner store to buy some Dutch Masters for some new exotic weed he just copped from the Heights. Andy hopped out the Porsche with the frog eyes with his swag on a million, dripped out in designer with a big Cuban link chain and a Rolex watch. Andy walked past a group of Dominicans posted up on the corner selling E pills and grams of coke.

"Yooo, papi, we got whatever you need over here, you heard?" one of the Dominicans said.

"Good looks, fam, but I'm straight," Andy said before walking into the small corner store, which was blasting loud Latina music.

Andy felt funny stares from two young Spanish niggas in the back behind the counter looking at him. After he paid for his items, he turned to leave, and when he looked in the store's mirrored ceiling, he saw the two young Spanish cats with guns in their hands coming back at him. The store clerk went in the back, locking the door.

Andy played it smooth, waiting until they got closer, and then fired seven rounds, killing one of them and seriously injuring the other. Andy saw the other one trying to crawl away, but Andy was on his ass.

"You bitch-ass nigga!" Andy shouted, kicking him in his ass. "Who sent you? Because I know I don't look sweet, homie," Andy said, putting his gun to the kid head.

"Melissa told us you was Flaco's killer and she dropped a bag on your head," he said

"Who the fuck is Melissa?"

"Flaco——"

Four gunmen ran into the store before he could finish his sentence and with Andy blowing his brains out, it didn't help. Andy ran down the small aisle and fired rounds at the gunmen, hitting one of them in the shoulder. Bullets were hitting canned food, chips, cookies, and bread as Andy tried to get low and fire back, hitting two of them in the face. The last gunman ran out of the store. One was still alive with a shoulder injury, but he took off also. Andy ran out of the store and made it outside to see that the block was clear. He climbed in the Porsche, racing off to hear gunshots, but none hit the car.

Andy's mind was racing as he tried to figure out who the fuck Melissa was and how she had the drop on him. He remembered when he robbed Flaco and killed his people, but then it hit him like a brick. He heard Flaco had a sister somewhere, but it never crossed his mind to look into it because he had a lot going on at the moment.

Now he regretted not looking into whoever his sister was.

***

Long Island, NY

Mr. Nicolas Grant had been one of the head DA's in Brooklyn for over twenty-five years. He retired two months ago so he could spend time with his wife fishing and traveling the world. Mr. Grant was an older white man in his early sixties with seven kids and four grandchildren. His wife was an ex-school teacher. She was the same age as him, but she took care of herself by exercising daily and eating healthy.

"Baby, are you sure we should sail out this early?" Mrs. Grant asked as they made their way down the boat dock area to their small boat they rented for the day.

"It will be nice later, trust me. I can't wait to catch some good red snapper. I've been dreaming about it all last night, love." Mr. Grant saw a beautiful woman ahead who looked like she was having a little trouble untying her anchor so she could drop it in the water.

"She looks like she could use some help," Mrs. Grant stated in her sweet old lady voice.

"Excuse me, Miss, do you need some help?" Mr. Grant asked, taking off his fisherman hat, trying not to look at her phat ass - the type he only saw on TV.

"Yes please. I'm trying to go for a sail, but it seems like this rope won't get loose," she said, still trying to loosen the thick rope.

"Let me up. I been doing this for some time," Mr. Grant said, switching positions with her, smelling her strong perfume. Mr. Grant wished his wife could smell like this instead of musk.

BOOM!

The loud noise scared Mr. Grant. He looked behind him to see a hole in his wife's head and then her body being kicked into the water by the beautiful Spanish woman named Maryanna.

BOOM! BOOM! BOOM!

Mr. Grant took three bullets from a .357 to the face before his body slumped into the back of the small boat.

Maryanna walked off with another mission complete.

Chapter 22

San Quentin Prison, Cali

Ruiz had just received the incoming mail under his door and it was from his daughter. Ruiz had recently put in a new appeal to get off of death row and back in general population. He was on the tier with terrorists, serial killers, rapists, crazy murderers and madmen. His execution date was in three more years and he would prefer to be dead than to be on the range. Hearing grown men talk to themselves all day, yelling and screaming, would make anybody hang themselves. In the last two months, six death row inmates had hanged themselves.

Ruiz opened the letter from Paola, which was sent from a New York area code.

"Dear Dad,
I've been a little busy lately so I'm sorry for not reaching out but I hope my letter finds you in good spirits. Mommy is gone and now Mario. When I find out who is behind this, Father, I swear on my soul I will destroy everything they love and some. I'm trying to handle what I came out here to do but it's hard because my target has a lot going on. But I will handle all of my affairs in a matter of months. I formed a plan that I believe will work. I have a lot of new friends to help the family grow. I'ma end this. Hope to hear from you soon. Take care.
Love you.

Ruiz took off his reading glasses, thinking about Paola. She was talking reckless in the letter, but he excused that. He hoped she was safe and okay. He meant to warn her about Rita, but he hadn't spoken to Paola yet. He didn't want her doing any type of business with her because she was poison. He also wondered what she meant by new friends. He taught her well to never trust a New Yorker because they would cross you faster than an enemy.

Little did Ruiz know that Rita and Paola were deep in business and making millions together. The envelope didn't have a return address, so he couldn't write back.

***

Newburgh, NY

Spice was parked behind a project building near the hospital, which was known for its high drug trafficking. He was in the driver's seat of his Audi A8 with his hands behind his head, watching Orianna suck the life out of his dick.

"Ummm," he moaned.

"Cum down my throat," she said, going deep on his dick, sticking out her tongue like a true freak. She slurped on his wet dick, making all types of noise as she twisted her head and neck, working her thick lips.

"I'm about to cum, ma." Spice watched her deep throat his man at a fast pace without gagging.

She looked at him with her puppy dog eyes until he shot a load down her throat. She swallowed every drop like a big girl. Orianna came up from wiping her mouth, smiling, knowing she put in some work just now, but she had plans for when they got back to the hotel.

"You stepped your game up. That was four minutes and two seconds," Spice said, checking out his Rolex watch.

"I been practicing."

"I can tell. But how's everything with the kids and your job?" Spice asked, pulling out from behind the projects.

"I'm okay, I guess, but since Rell died, life been hard. The Feds keep coming to my house asking questions, and I don't know nothing. If I did, I would tell them," she said as Spice gave her a dirty look.

"When niggas play in theses streets, ma, they only get one thing as an outcome."

"What? Well, if someone kills someone I love I'ma tell on them," Orianna said with no shame.

The Audi pulled into the hotel parking lot and parked.
Boc! Boc! Boc! Boc!
Spice shot Orianna in the head and kicked her out of the car.
Spice rode in silence back home, thinking about what he had to do to Orianna because he knew she was a liability.

***

Upper Westside, NY

Rita and Paola were leaving a fancy upper class restaurant, where they discussed business arrangements for the next shipment in two days.

"Thanks for everything once again," Rita told Paola as a bunch of goons followed behind them outside.

"Sure. I see you're constant, and my pops speaks highly of you."

"When have you spoken to Ruiz?" Rita asked.

"It's been a while, but I recently wrote him to see how he was doing."

"Oh, okay," Rita stated, thinking about how Ruiz almost killed her in L.A.

Before Paola could respond, three vans pulled up and niggas hopped out shooting, taking out most of their guards. Wolf and Andy tried to get Rita and Paola, but they were hiding behind their cars and guards.

The guards were in a vicious toe-to-toe gun battle. Wolf ducked bullets from Rita, trying to get Paola. Six guards were on Andy's line. Two GMC SUV trucks pulled up and more goons hopped out of them. Julie was leading them. Julie was shooting towards Paola, taking out three of her shooters. Wolf and Andy looked at each other, wondering who she was, because she was knocking niggas down like a trained assassin.

A cop car pulled up and Paola shot through the window, hitting the officer seven times. The gun battle didn't stop, but Rita and

Paola were running out of men so they both hopped in a truck with the two shooters who were left standing.

Wolf wasn't trying to let them get away, but two more cop cars pulled up. The cops hopped out shooting and Julie aired them out, killing both cops. Wolf and Andy looked around, saw all the dead bodies, and had to leave but they both looked at Julie and how sexy she was before getting inside the vans and speeding out of the packed lot. Julie was behind them.

Chapter 23

Auburn Maximum Security Prison, NY
Weeks later

CB was on the visit room floor, waiting for OG Chuck to come out. CB remembered these days when he used to come down for visits to catch the pack so he and his homies could make some money and be straight while bidding in the belly of the beast. He was going to bring Bella with him, but she had to take care of something important, so he drove by himself for seven hours.

Things since Rell's death had been rocky because he had to find new workers. Yonkers was already flooded with Andy's workers. CB was starting to see that every block selling weight was all selling for Andy.

His mom told him about the shootout she had with Wolf, Andy, and some Spanish bitch. It was all she talked about for two weeks. Rita blamed CB for not taking care of Andy and Wolf like she asked him to. CB's attention had been elsewhere, mainly on Isabella and money. He tried to explain to his mom that he had just come home from doing all that time and he was enjoying life, but she went off on him. CB promised her he would tighten up and take care of Andy and Wolf ASAP.

CB saw OG walk through the heavy metal door smiling. They had talked yesterday so OG knew he was coming to see him and he couldn't wait.

"What's popping, old man?"

"Old man? Don't let this old man walk trick you, young blood," OG said, giving CB a tight hug before sitting down across from him. OG placed his hands on the table. It was a new role the prison had after an inmate recently pulled a knife out of his ass and stabbed his baby mother twenty-four times, killing her.

"How you holding up in there? I sent Ra Balla a pack up here with a little Spanish bitch I met in the club last week. Did he hit your hand?" CB asked, referring to the stripper bitch he sent up with six ounces of dope and weed in loonies for OG.

"Hell yeah, I got that. I was waiting at his cell door for him to come back. I even stood there and watched him shit it all out, listened to everything that hit the toilet water," OG said seriously. CB knew OG wasn't lying because he was serious about his money and business. He took morals and honor seriously.

"A'ight, good."

"How's life for you? I got your pics and I see you in big jewelry, foreign cars...and who's the beautiful girl? I showed a couple of your homies and they were all hyped up," OG stated.

"I'm living a fair life. That's Isabella, my wifey. I can't lie, she may be the one," CB said, smiling just thinking about her.

"Good. I'm proud of you. But I have something I've been meaning to tell you for a long time," OG said, taking a deep breath, knowing it was now or never.

"What's up?"

"I'm...your father."

CB laughed, thinking OG was giving himself too much credit, but CB did look at him as a father figure. "I will always look at you as a father, OG. What's understood never has to be said."

"No, no, you don't understand. I'm your birth father. Me and Rita been holding this back from you, Black, and Victoria for years."

"What? This can't be. You was in jail?"

"I came to prison after Victoria was born. CB, when you were a kid, Rita used to come to Brooklyn where I was living a crazy life and she kept getting pregnant, but she didn't want me around y'all, especially after the home invasion where she almost lost her last son. Your mom came to see me a couple of months ago, thinking it was time to tell you the truth, but I didn't have the balls to do it."

"So when I came here, you knew all along. That's why you kept me close and got me moved next door to you." CB's mind was spinning

"Yes. I'm sorry you had to find out like this so late, but things got bad when I came to prison. My empire fell, Rita robbed me, and she told the police on me and took the stand on me at my trial date. She was the main witness. I have all the paperwork. Since she had y'all, I left her be, but she had another child on me anyway, the Wolf kid. I knew nothing about it until I came to prison. She can't be trusted, CB. Your mom is a deadly dangerous woman."

"I have to go," CB said, getting up to leave because it was too much to take in at once. He couldn't believe OG had just dropped a bomb on him.

***

Bronx, NY

Force had just come from looking at a two-story house in a nice area next to the Bronx Zoo. It was time to get out of Yonkers because too much shit was going on, and Force refused to get caught slipping where he laid his head at. Force had recently copped a new Jaguar to get low in until he found something he really liked, but winter was right around the corner and a Benz G-Wagon was on his mind.

He pulled up behind a public city bus blasting a Pop Smoke album, feeling his energy and music. In an hour he was supposed to meet Demon in Harlem to go put in some work. Since Demon's sister got killed at her college, Demon had been depressed. Force felt his pain. Demon's sister was a bad little bitch. Force tried to fuck, but she curved him every time. Force wanted answers about who Melissa was because she wanted Andy dead and he needed to get the drop on her for Andy. That's why he was going out to Harlem.

A black Range with tints pulled up on the side of him, but Force didn't pay the SUV any mind until shots rang out into his car. Force ducked and put the car in reverse, backing up only ten feet before slamming into a Honda SUV with two old white people inside. Before the Range could back up, Force was out of his car firing broad daylight

Boc! Boc! Boc! Boc! Boc! Boc! Boc! Boc!

Force continued to shoot into the Range even when it pulled off into traffic with bullet holes through the back door and windows.

Glass was shattered all over the place when Force got back inside his Jag, which was fucked up on the driver's side. There were so many bullet holes in his door panel he could play connect the dots.

Force took the back blocks, parked the Jag in someone's driveway, and called Demon to come pick him up because he had three guns in the trunk. If he was to get pulled over, he would be going away a long time.

During the shootout, Force saw two Jamaican flags on the headrest of the seats, so he knew who sent the hit. Force knew when he caught up to Mad Max, he wasn't going to miss again.

Chapter 24

Queens, NY

Club Angel was jam-packed tonight for the stripper show down, which was when the hottest strippers in the city battled on stage. The dancers were having twerking contests, squirting contests, deep throating contests, and whatever else the crowd desired.

Force was front row with two young boys from his block tossing money and popping bottles, celebrating Force's birthday. Tory Lanez's new song was booming through the club speakers as four bad Spanish strippers were on stage on the floor shaking their asses, making the crowd go crazy.

"Shake that shit!" Force yelled, seeing one of the bitches twerking so hard her ass turned red.

Force and his crew tossed stacks of money until their arms started to hurt. An hour later, Force was tipsy off Ace of Spade when he saw Audrey number pop up.

Audrey was home waiting for him and she said she had a surprise for him. She had been walking around the crib looking like a snack. He never knew she had an ass on her until he saw her in booty shorts. She and Force had been getting real close and their vibes were so strong it made the both of them wonder if they could be soul mates.

Force left the club, taking in the fresh air because the club was hot and muggy.

"I tossed almost ten racks, son. Never again on them stank pussy bitches," Lil Ton said upset he ain't get no pussy.

"How you know how they pussy smell?" Pawn asked him, tapping Force, laughing.

"Nigga, the whole club smelled like a whore house on Dyckman, nigga, what the fuck you talking about?" Lil Ton replied, walking through the packed car lot in the back of the club.

Boc! Boc! Boc! Boc! Boc! Boc! Boc!

Lil Ton's body was riddled with bullets out of nowhere. Force and Pawn got low with their guns drawn, clapping back at the four niggas they saw moving through the large parking lot. Force hit one of the gunmen in the neck

"Yo Pawn. Pawn!" Force looked behind him to see Pawn on the ground with a hole in his head and a gunman pointing a pistol at him.

"This from Trigger," the masked man stated with his finger on the trigger.

"Fuck you," Force said with a smirk, ready to die like the Biggie song.

Tat-tat-tat-tat-tat-tat!

So many bullets hit the gunman at once that his body spun around before hitting the ground. Then the shooter shot at the two other gunmen a few feet away, who looked spooked before they each caught a head shot.

Force looked up at the shooter and smiled, seeing her with double vision because he was still fucked up from drinking all that Ace in the club.

"Come on, birthday boy. This is why you should have stayed home with me," Audrey said, grabbing his hand. She was dressed in a black outfit and a black hat and carrying her Draco.

"Where you come from?" Force asked, getting inside her Lexus, pulling out the back entrance so the civilians coming out the front of the club wouldn't see them.

"You stank. You smell like them hoes. And if you must know, I was coming to check on you because you ain't text or call me back, so I thought something happened to your crazy ass," she said, getting on the highway, heading home.

"So what's the surprise?"

"You will see after we get home and you get in the shower," she replied.

"You mean together?" he said in a raspy voice.

"What you think? Of course! I just hope you can handle it, papi," she said, not hearing him reply. She called his name, thinking he was asleep, then saw blood leaking from his red and black Dior shirt.

"Shit." She checked for a pulse and he still had one so he was alive. Audrey was a pro in the medical field thanks to the Navy. When she was in Iraq and Iran, she saved a lot of lives so she knew what to do.

Once she got home, she carried Force inside and gave him some medicine to keep him alive as she took the bullet out of his side. After twenty minutes of working on him he was alive, but still asleep. The alcohol saved his life. She put him to bed and watched him sleep as she laid next to him. She had never felt this way about a man. She knew she was out here on a mission and couldn't be distracted, but Force was stealing her heart.

***

San Quentin Prison, Cali

Julie looked at the huge prison that sat on the edge of the water and pushed all of her fears out of her thought process. Today she was coming to see Ruiz for answers she had been yearning for for years. She walked through the large gates after being scanned. She spent over thirty minutes inside the jail going through the visitor phases, which was the guards giving inmates family and friends problems to discourage them from coming back to visit them.

Two guards brought her to the death row visit area, which was filled with booths with phones and barbed wire in the window. Julie waited with her legs crossed wondering what to say to the man who had her family murdered in cold blood. Minutes later she saw an older Spanish man walk out. He had glasses and a nice build. When he was being unshackled by the prison guard he looked her in her eyes, already knowing who she was.

"You look just like your mother," Ruiz stated, picking up the phone.

"The one you killed," she said, giving him a menacing look. If looks could kill, Ruiz would be dead.

"So you come for answers? I have nothing to hide, Julie," Ruiz already knew her name and the relationship she had with Sousa, but he kept it to himself. Sousa was too slow and blinded by her beauty to really know who she was and what she was there for.

"Yes."

"Me and your mother had something very special before your father came into the picture. Your father killed my uncle, the man who raised me and my brothers. I believe in revenge, so to sum up the story, I had Sousa pay your family a little visit after they both crossed me. Your grandfather was the power behind your father's cartel and still is, but I fear no man."

Julie never remembered her grandfather being a cartel boss. All she remembered was him having four farms and a lot of acres, so it was new news to her. "Thank you for the closure," she said, now ready to leave because she had everything she came for.

"You're welcome. Have fun in New York."

"I will. And Ruiz? Your wife's and son's cries were like music to my ears. I can't wait to hear Paola's."

"You little bitch! I will——" Ruiz shouted.

Julie walked out of the booth as he yelled. Ruiz now knew who was responsible for his family's deaths.

Chapter 25

Lower East Side, NY
Weeks later

"Uhhhh, shitttt, yessss, Andy!" Mia screamed with her legs on his shoulders.

Andy long stroked in her, hearing the gushy noise every time he went in and out. Mia's pussy was so good that Andy had to fuck her slow because if he was to go any faster, then he would erupt in her.

"Oh God," she moaned as he ripped her walls open, causing her lower body to shake while her pussy contracted and clenched on his dick. She grabbed a pillow behind her and pressed it to her mouth to muffle her loud screams of pleasure because the dick was popping. Her inner walls tightened as she caught her orgasm on her satin sheets. Andy felt her hips jerk upwards.

"Ah, ah, ah, yesss! Mmm!" she screamed, making Andy finally nut as her tight pussy gripped his dick.

"Damn, I need a break and cigs," Mia said, feeling chills throughout her body.

"Tell me you like this dick," Andy said, standing there naked with his dick swinging.

"I love it," she said, placing her lips on the tip, kissing it like a trophy prize.

"I'm tired, ma. You put it down on a nigga," Andy said thinking about how they fucked all around her nice clean condo overseeing the city.

"I want you to fuck me from the back again. I like to feel you in my stomach," she said as he looked at her sexy body, getting a hard-on again.

Andy looked at the flat screen TV then at her dresser, seeing a photo of her and three other kids at an amusement park

"Who is this?" Andy asked, looking at the photo.

"Me and my brothers when we were kids," Mia said, taking the picture frame and placing it inside her dresser drawer.

"Why you never talk about them?" he asked.

"Some things I just don't like talking about. You gotta respect that. I have to use the bathroom. Why don't you go pour us some more drinks so we can get round six popping. You got a bitch horny and ready," she said, getting up and walking to the bathroom.

Andy threw on some boxer briefs and went to the bar in the dining room area to make drinks for them, wondering why she switched up on him real quick, but he respected boundaries.

***

Manhattan, NY

Paola was in a nail salon getting her nails and feet done. It'd been a while because she had been so busy with hunting Wolf and taking care of the family business she had no time for herself.

She hadn't been able to sleep since the last time she saw Wolf and she couldn't deny how wet she got seeing him. Her wedding ring was still on her hand. She refused to take it off because it meant a lot to her still.

Five guards were waiting outside the glass windows. The Korean woman was painting her toes pink and white with small designs on them, just like her manicured nails. Paola laid her head back in the chair, getting peace of mind. Then the havoc started.

Boom! Boom! Boom! Boom! Boom!

Boc! Boc! Boc! Boc! Boc!

Paola saw her guards getting crashed by ten men dressed in army fatigue outfits

"Muthafuckers!" Paola yelled when five gunmen along with Julie rushed inside, shooting everybody in sight. Paola was quick on her feet with her pistol in hand, firing at the guards, taking two of them out with clean shots to the chest.

Boom! Boom! Boom! Boom! Boom!

Julie fired a double barrel 12 gauge toward Paola's head, watching her dive to the floor barefoot.

"I'ma kill you, little whore!" Julie yelled, seeing Paola crawl toward a table.

Boc! Boc! Boc! Boc! Boc!

Paola popped up, shooting at Julie but hitting one of her guards instead. Paola saw three more men enter the front, shooting like old western cowboys, killing seven civilians. There was a back exit sign and Paola went for it at full speed.

"Get her!" Julie yelled like a madwoman to her goon when she saw Paola trying to get away.

Julie fired the shotgun at her, almost hitting Paola in the back. The shotgun put big holes in the wall as gunsmoke filled the nail salon.

Paola made it out the back door safe and secure, running down the alleyway until she made it to a main street, where she hopped in a cab barefoot, fucking up her manicured feet. Her heart was racing at a fast pace. The cab driver asked where she was going, but her eardrums were fucked up from the loud gunfire.

Romell Tukes

Chapter 26

Bridgeport, CT

Force was healed up and back to his regular self, thanks to Audrey's help. Force didn't even know he was shot on his birthday until he woke up the next day and Audrey was standing over him. When she told him what happened the night before, he remembered one of the shooters saying Trigger's name before Audrey popped out of the cut. Force and Lil Tom, who was Trigger's little brother, were best friends so he knew a lot about Trigger from what Lil Tom used to tell him. What Trigger didn't know was that his little brother was fucking his baby mother.

Lil Tom had Force with him one day in Connecticut to chill with Trigger's baby mama and her friend and they ended up fucking. Force remembered where Trigger's BM lived in Bridgeport so he was currently parked down the block watching the house, thinking of a plan.

***

Amira was cleaning her house, waiting on her two daughters to be dropped off by her mother. Last night she had a small get-together and she woke up to three niggas in her bed. Amira was a party girl and a big freak. Needless to say, she was down for whatever.

She was from Atlanta, but had moved to Connecticut after having two children by Trigger. They met in an Atlanta strip club, where she was working at the time trying to pay for college. When she met Trigger, her life changed for the better. He took her out of the clubs and gave her a good life. He moved her out of Atlanta.

Amira was beautiful at 5'3", 150 pounds, with thick thighs, a big bubble ass, and long braids. She was high yellow with tattoos all over her ass and a flat stomach that looked like an ironing board.

Hearing the doorbell ring took her out of her cleaning zone. She stopped cleaning the kitchen floor, which smelled like Pine Sol, to go get the door, thinking it was her daughters. Her body was sore and her ass was hurting, so she walked on her toes. Upon opening the door, she saw Lil Tom's friend who had come by a couple of times a while back.

"Force?"

"Hey Amira."

"What are you doing here?" she asked, surprised to see him. But she couldn't front; he was looking sexy in his tight designer shirt.

"I was nearby at a friend's house and I remembered you lived here, so I just wanted to say hi," he said looking at the phat pussy print busting out of the front of her shorts.

"Awwwwww that's so cute! Um, come in. I'm just waiting on my mom to drop my kids off. Last night was crazy," Amira said, walking inside in front of him, giving him a good view of her wide ass, which she got done in DR years ago.

"How you been? This is a nice house. Looks like you did some changing," Force said, looking at the new all-white living room area.

"Glad someone notices!" she yelled from the kitchen.

"Your baby father been around? I haven't seen him lately," Force asked, seeing her come out the kitchen with two beers.

"I think he's in New York. That nigga don't even come check on his kids, but he drops off that money twice a month so I can live like a boss bitch and take care of his kids," she said shamelessly.

"I saw your pink BMW i8 out front."

"Facts," she said, sitting next to him, opening her beer, feeling her pussy get moist.

"You looking good." Force looked at her body then her juicy lips.

"Thanks. It could be yours if you say the word."

"Oh yeah?"

"Yeah," she said, inching towards him to kiss him. But her breath smelled like last night. She had been sucking so much dick and drinking niggas' cum like water.

Force smelled the powerful odor from her mouth and pulled the other way. "I have to go, but I'll be back," he said, standing up.

"So you about to play hard to get, huh? Just let me taste it. I bet I can change your mind," she said, reaching for his Louis Vuitton belt buckle.

Force pulled out his pistol and shot her in her forehead twice, then walked out towards the front to see an older woman and two little girls coming up the stairs. When they saw Force coming out of the house, they froze.

"Grandmom, who is he?" one of the little girls asked.

"Excuse me?" the old lady asked Force before he pulled out his gun from his back, shooting her four times in the chest.

The two little girls stood there, unaware what just happened.

"Go upstairs and when the police come, tell them a white man did this to your family, okay?" Force told both of the little girls as they nodded their heads.

***

Yonkers, NY

Demon came out of the woods in the park where he had practiced his devil worshipping acts for years. He lived a block away so he tried to come out here every other night around 11:15 p.m. so he could talk to his demons.

He felt something was off tonight. He heard a noise coming from the bushes and reached for his weapon, but he was too late.

Bullets from seven different guns hopped out of the bushes, firing at Demon, but he wasn't going out like no sucker. He fired his Glock, hitting three shooters. Everybody had dreads in their heads so he knew Mad Max was behind this. Demon ran out of bullets because he had left his thirty round clip in the crib.

Demon ran into the dark woods, dodging bullets. He knew the dread heads would never be able to find him in the deep woods at this time of the night.

Romell Tukes

Chapter 27

Hudson River, NY

Andy had rented a small yacht for the evening for his date with Maryanna. He had the lower deck set up with a nice candlelight vibe and he had two personal chiefs servicing a gourmet meal. Maryanna rocked a red Chanel strapless dress with high heels and Andy rocked a black Armani suit, looking like a black Bill Gates.

"This shit is crazy, Andy. I must say I never been on one of these," Maryanna stated, looking around at the nice set-up he had put together.

"It's a special night for me, Maryanna. I been waiting to get up with you," he said, looking into her beautiful eyes.

"You're so cute! But I don't know if you really ready for a woman like me."

"That's your excuse for why you been ducking me?"

"I wasn't ducking you. I was just focused on something important."

"That makes two of us. But fuck all that. We here now and I want you," he stated.

"How bad?" she said sexually, drinking wine.

"Let me show you," he said, standing up and walking over to her. Andy lifted her up from her seat and moved everything off the table. He sat her on the edge and lifted her dress up, feeling her thick thighs.

"Mmmmmm," she moaned as he sucked on her neck.

One thing led to the next and then Andy had his dick in her warm, moist pussy, slowly spreading her pussy lips open.

"Ohhhhh," she moaned wildly, feeling him tear her pussy walls open. She hadn't gotten dick in years so she was open the moment the tip entered her.

When Andy got himself halfway in her pussy, the pussy walls weren't opening. She was too tight. "Loosen up," he said as she relaxed her pussy muscles.

Minutes later, she was grinding her hips on his dick going crazy.

"Damn," Andy said, now deep in her love box, which was squeezing his dick with her tight vise grip.

Maryanna came hard on his dick and Andy came with her.

"Can we go to the room?" she said, dizzy, legs shaking. She was horny and ready for more.

Andy picked her up and brought her to the bedroom and enjoyed a long night of hot, passionate sex.

***

Yonkers, NY

Wolf saw CB and Bella coming out of the phone store, smiling and holding each other's hands. It wasn't hard to find CB around Yonkers because he was still selling weight and making moves.

The block was empty and Wolf saw the perfect time to bust his move. He pulled his ski mask down and hopped out with his Desert Eagle in hand.

***

CB and Isabella had just come from buying the new iPhones that had dropped. Their love life was good and everything was perfect.

"You wanna go to the car dealership to get the Benz, baby?" CB asked Bella.

"Yeah, it should be there today, daddy," she said, seeing a man crossing the street with a mask.

Bella wasn't dumb. It was 11 a.m. and it wasn't cold enough for a mask. "Baby, I think——"

Boc! Boc! Boc!

Bella ducked and CB pulled out his gun, busting at the masked man. Bella tried to run, but a bullet hit her in the left shoulder. CB saw this and sprayed round after round, backing the gunman down.

The masked man took off his mask and CB was shocked to see Wolf.

Bo Boc! Boc! Boc! Boc!

Wolf wasn't letting up. He saw CB trying to get Bella inside the BMW. CB fired five more rounds at Wolf, who hid behind a commercial truck.

CB saw the perfect chance to get away and take Isabella to the hospital. Wolf saw the BMW speeding off down the block. "Fuck!" Wolf yelled, walking off to his car.

***

Brooklyn, NY
Days later

Wolf had spoken to Andy last night about Mad Max and he wanted to take care of the Rasta. He knew Andy and his crew would prolong the situation, which could become a nasty outcome.

He was dressed in a Muslim garment with a kufi with a stack of Qurans in his hand as if he was selling them. It was a little chilly outside today because winter was days away, and a winter in New York was nothing to play with at all. Wolf walked up and down the block in the Crown Heights section of Brooklyn, where there was a big Muslim community, just like the Bed-Stuy area.

***

Mad Max walked outside of one of the Golden Caribbean restaurants he owned with four big Rastas by his side. He had to drop off some work to one of his clients in Staten Island, his man Dex. He wanted thirty-five joints.

Mad Max had been laying low, but he had been sending his goons at Force, Andy, and Demon. He kept coming up short, which was not like him.

Looking a few feet away from him, he saw a Muslim man selling Qurans, which was a regular sight in Brooklyn.

"Qurans... Qurans!" the man shouted as Mad Max opened up the truck door.

Tat-tat-tat-tat-tat-tat-tat-tat-tat-tat!

Mad Max caught two shots to the head and five to his back, leaving his body slumped in the truck. Wolf shot his four guards with the 100 round Draco in his hand, chopping them down before they had a chance to get to their weapons.

Wolf saw his job was now completed, but when he turned around, an SK assault rifle with a knife attached to the end was pointed at his face. When he saw Paola's face behind the weapon with real tears in her eyes, he didn't know what to do because it was an awkward position.

"Why, Romeo?" was all she could say with tears. "Why kill my father?"

"Why try to kill me to please a man who was never there for you?"

"You don't know shit about my father!" she yelled like a crazy bitch in a nuthouse would at the nurses.

"What I do know is the love I had for you was real - until you crossed me - so if you're going to kill me, do it," Wolf said, dropping his Draco on the ground.

Before she could reply, she saw a woman and a group of shooters coming from the side block.

Tat-tat-tat-tat-tat-tat-tat-tat!

Paola shot a couple of the shooters before looking at Wolf in his soft eyes that read through her soul. She ran the opposite way, towards where she came from, because there were close to twenty shooters firing at her. Wolf was about to fire back until he saw Salma coming his way.

"What's good, papi? Did I break up the ceremony?" she asked, giving him a jealous look. She walked up to him and kissed his lips.

"Why are you here?" Wolf asked, walking to his car with her by his side. He couldn't lie; she was looking sexy with a gun, dressed in a designer sweat suit with Timbs on. She was looking like a real New York bitch.

"I was following her - following you, papi. I just saved your life and I don't get a thank you? It's like you fucked me and dumped me. I don't give up the goodies unless you're mine."

"I don't belong to nobody. Get the fuck away from my car," Wolf said, climbing in his car, upset about what happened.

Salma wanted to shoot him for disrespecting her, but she laughed it off and let him pull off. She was really crushed because she felt like she was in love with him.

Romell Tukes

Chapter 28

Sleepy Hollow, NY

Isabella was in her apartment, lying on her couch and watching *Basketball Wives* on her large flat screen TV in her living room. She had a brace on her left arm due to her shoulder injury. Bella couldn't believe Wolf shot her. She couldn't believe it was him because there hadn't been a day that went past she didn't think about him. Since the shooting, she hadn't talked about what happened because she knew what type of life CB was into, but him beefing with the man who killed her father and who she used to be in love with had been heavy on her mind.

When CB dropped her off at the hospital, he couldn't stay because he knew police would be lurking. Bella told the police, who remembered her from the force when she was a cop, that she was driving and got hit by a stray bullet.

CB walked out of the kitchen with a plate of pizza he had just ordered for her from Pizza Hut.

"Thank you, babe."

"You welcome," CB said, sitting next to her putting her feet on his lap.

"Can I ask you something?" She turned off the TV with the digital remote.

"Yeah. What's up, ma?"

"Who was that kid who shot me?"

"Oh, baby, don't worry about that. I'ma take care of it. Don't worry yourself."

"It's not about that, CB. He is very dangerous," she said, getting CB's full attention.

"How do you know that?"

"You remember when I told you a man killed my father, the FBI agent?"

"Yes."

"It was him. Wolf."

"My brother killed your dad?" CB said in shock.

"Your brother? You can't be serious," she said, now sitting up
"Yeah, he's my brother. Sorry I didn't tell you."
"CB, your brother is my ex-boyfriend," she said, seeing an awkward look on CB's face.
"Wow, you're the cop chick. How the fuck I ain't put two and two together?" CB shouted.
"This is too much. I'ma go for a walk," Bella said, getting up to leave, feeling all types of emotions because she had fallen in love with her ex-lover's brother.

***

Williamsburg, Brooklyn

Officer Tisadle was a thirty year vet on the NYPD force. He was a sergeant and one of the most respected policemen in Brooklyn. He was sixty-two years old and still in the battlefield, patrolling the streets trying to make it safer for families, children, and civilians. Sergeant Tisadle had a beautiful wife and four grown children with families of their own.

It was a cold winter day outside so the streets were empty. He was driving his patrol car and saw a woman in an alley on the ground, holding her leg as if it was broken. Sergeant Tisadle could tell she needed help, so he parked his unit car and got out to help her.

"Miss, are you okay? What's wrong?" Sergeant Tisadle asked, approaching her, trying to be helpful to the beautiful Spanish woman.

She didn't say a word. She pulled out a pistol from under her leg and shot Sergeant Tisadle in the head five times. His body dropped in the snow, staining the snow red.

Maryanna sneaked out of the alley, placing her Louis Vuitton hoodie over her head and walking down the block to her car.

Maryanna had been watching Sergeant Tisadle for three days, so she knew his routes. She came up with a quick plan when she saw him coming to reel him in, and it worked.

***

Westchester, NY

Rita was waiting on Trigger to arrive for their meeting. She had extra guards trained to kill surrounding her property after what her son Wolf did to the last group.

She was looking like a snack in her tight white Fendi dress with Fendi pumps and her curves were poking out, showing enough to make anyone lust in the house of God.

She was in her library when Trigger's Bentley pull into her driveway. She glanced at herself in the mirror, looking at her big butt, smacking it, then fixing her hair placed in a bun. When she made her way downstairs, Trigger was standing in the hall staring at her body and beauty. He had never seen her look so good.

"Trigger, let's go to my office," she said, taking him to the private downstairs office she used to file paperwork and hold small meetings. "Thanks for coming. How's business?" she asked, sitting in a couch across from him

"Fair. But these niggas are becoming a headache. They killed my baby mother and her mom. I'm just glad they left the kids out of this."

"I'm sorry to hear that. It will all work out. They have too many enemies. Mad Max was killed, so now we have to push harder to get them out the way," she said, catching Trigger looking up her nice smooth, brown, thick legs.   "You like what you see?"

"Hell yeah", Trigger said, seeing her opening her legs a little more, seeing she had on no panties.

"Watch this," she said, opening the dresser and pulling out a big fourteen inch black dildo. She popped out her titties and cocked her legs wide open, exposing her phat bold pussy, which was dripping.

Trigger's eyes were wide open as he watched her place the biggest vibrator he had ever seen down her gushiness.

"Ummmmm," she moaned, shoving the toy all the way down her pussy, then pulling it out to show how her creamy cum coated the vibrator

"Dammnnn!"

"Your turn," she said, smiling, seeing him strip naked and make his way to her. His thick dick was hard when he entered her, stretching her walls open as he started pounding her pussy out.

"Ooooooooh shit! Fuck!" she screamed while he sucked on her nipples, getting deep in her soaking wet warm pussy.

The juices from her pussy ran down her ass while he continued to fuck the life outta her, showing he had enough stamina to go for days. The pleasure she was receiving made her want to scream, but she just let him pound her out until they both came.

Trigger went down south and licked her swollen clit gently, savoring her sweetness, making slurping sounds as her body quivered and she tried to catch her breath.

"Eat that pussy, baby, fuck! I'm cumming!" she said, cumming hard like a waterfall and he savored every drop.

"You taste good," he said, turning her over on her side, sliding his dick into her from behind and violently thrusting himself in and out of her ass.

"Uhhh…yessss…harder!" she screamed while he rammed his dick into her. When he came deep inside her asshole, she rode his dick until she climaxed, then it was over.

They ate dinner and talked business.

Chapter 29

Beacon, NY

"Check, can you hear me, bro?" Force said through his walkie-talkie, talking to Demon, who was parked down the block waiting on their target so they could make their moves.

"I hear you, nigga. How loud do you have to yell?" Demon shouted back into his earpiece.

"You like a grumpy old man, son. You need to cheer up, fam," Force told him.

"If you lived the life I did, you would be the same," Demon replied.

Force didn't say shit back because he knew Demon's story better than anybody and he had a fucked-up life. "Let's focus, son. I think that's your man right there," Force said, watching Trigger come out of the two-story house where his mom lived. Andy gave Force all the info he needed to get Trigger out of the way because he was becoming a headache.

"It looks like he got three with him. This will be too easy," Demon stated, talking out loud.

"He's in the truck." Force watched the Tahoe truck pull out of the driveway in the middle class neighborhood. "It's on you now, bro," Force told Demon, seeing the Tahoe fly down the suburban street.

"Okay, copy," Demon said, following the truck in his Camaro SS.

***

Force walked up to the doorstep of Trigger's mom's house and knocked twice. Seconds later, a short tiny old lady answered the door with a Holy Bible in her frail hand. Trigger's mom was an extreme church lady. She tried to raise Trigger and Lil Tom like that, but they picked the street life over Jesus Christ.

"Yes? I hope you have the Lord in your life, young man. Jesus loves you." Those were her first words, which made Force feel guilt for what he came to do.

"I'm sorry," Force said, pulling his gun from his backside.

"You are the child of Satan! You come into the Lord's house to inflict pain and death on the Lord, child. Jesus loves you, whoever you are. I see in your eyes you don't want to do this, so put the gun down and give your life to the Most High," she said, holding out her right hand.

Force stayed silent. He knew he needed God in his life, but tonight was just bad timing.

Boc! Boc! Boc! Boc! Boc!

Force turned her face into a target. When family members saw her face, it would be too unrecognizable for an open casket funeral.

***

Demon was behind Trigger's SUV on the highway, tailing them, but he had no clue where they were going so he placed the sirens he stole from an abandoned cop car in his windshield. Demon turned on the red and blue sirens, lighting up the dark highway, getting behind the Tahoe truck as they slowly got to the far right lane, pulling over.

***

"What the fuck? You was speeding again, you big dumb muthafucker?" Trigger told his driver and bodyguard.

"No, not this time. I don't know what happened, Trigger."

"Just be cool," Trigger said, looking in his rearview mirror to see a blue Camaro SS, which was weird because normally state troopers would pull people over on these back highways.

Trigger had eight keys in the back and five assault rifles. He knew if they got pinched, he wasn't taking no charges. He never ratted, but he had too much to lose now, especially with a plug like Rita, who was throwing keys at him.

"This nigga look young to you?" the driver asked, looking in the mirror at Demon approaching them with a gun in his hand. When Trigger saw this, he yelled for the driver to pull off, but it was too late. Bullets busted out the back window, killing the men in the backseat. The driver caught a dome shot. Trigger knew the guns were in the backseat and Demon was getting closer. Trigger pushed the driver out of the front seat and onto the ground outside, ducking bullets.

Bloc! Bloc! Bloc!

Demon was a couple of feet away from the truck but when the truck pulled off, he fired until the clip was empty, upset that he just missed the main target.

"He got away," Demon said, hopping in his Camaro SS. running his tires over Trigger's driver's head.

***

Newburgh, NY

Spice and Julie were at his place just chilling, drinking and playing card games. Julie loved Spice's company. The two made shit official weeks ago and now they were glued to each other. Julie felt like it was time to tell him the truth.

"Spice," Julie said, stopping the card game.

"Yeah, let me guess. You ready for me to put you to sleep?" he said, rubbing her toned smooth legs until he got to her booty shorts, loving every inch of her perfect body.

"Stop playing, papi, for real. Listen to me. I been hiding something from you and I have to tell you," she said, seeing the worried look on his face.

"What you mean?"

"I came to New York from Cali to find the person who is helping my opponents."

"I don't get it," Spice said, standing up.

"Okay, look, my ex-husband was killed by me with the help of Ryan and his son Wolf from out here. My ex was a part of a powerful drug ring and I took over his operations, but his boss's daughter Paola, who is Wolf's wife, is trying to take over and I'm trying to kill her. I want Cali to myself and she is the only thing in my way. I know it's her father's connection that's keeping her above water. She is trying to kill her own husband Wolf for whatever reason, but I want all of them dead so I can take over NY and Cali."

"Hold on, so you telling me you're a plug?"

"Yeah."

"So those are your men sitting in the van at the end of the block?" Spice asked, looking out his window.

"Yeah."

"Did you know I deal with Wolf's people?"

"No, not until recently when I saw you and Andy meet up," she said honestly.

"Why are you telling me this?"

"Because I'm in love with you and I want you to myself. You never have to worry about money or drugs. I have an endless supply. What's mine is yours," she said, standing up and walking over to him.

Spice was shocked. This was every hood's nigga dream to be fucking the plug. The only thing that didn't sit well with him was leaving Andy for dead because that was the bro.

"I love you too and I got you," he said, making her jump up and down.

Chapter 30

Yonkers, NY

Rita rode in the backseat of the Maybach with a GMC SUV behind her full of goons.

It was snowy outside today. Rita had a doctor appointment. She wasn't feeling well. She thought it could be the flu.

When she got to the doctor's office, she had her driver park in the front while her guard checked out the area. Rita didn't trust a soul, not even her own children, and she was playing for keeps now that everything had been brought to light.

Bloc, Bloc, Bloc, Bloc, Bloc, Bloc, Bloc, Bloc, Bloc!

BOOM, BOOM! Bloc, Bloc, Bloc, Bloc! Boom!

Rita looked out the window to see Wolf going hard, taking out her gunmen. Rita knew she couldn't fuck with Wolf because he was too well trained

"Drive! Drive! Drive!" she yelled to her driver, who was watching the show outside his window.

The Maybach pulled off, leaving four dead niggas behind. Wolf saw his mom speed off. He paid her no mind. He just wanted to send another message.

***

Washington Heights, NY

Trigger had another baby mother in the Heights he kept on the low because she was his everything. He had a seven-year-old daughter with Venessa. She was Dominican and Brazilian and eye candy and with her body done, she looked like a model for a magazine.

Shit had been so hacked for Trigger lately. He didn't have time to spend with his daughter, especially after losing his two boys. He was ready to go back to Atlanta. He was mad at himself for coming back to New York to lose everything he loved. Tonight he was going to have Venessa pack up so she and his daughter could come back to Atlanta with him.

Walking into the building lobby, he saw a couple of Dominican kids selling drugs to some random person he didn't even know, just trying to get a dollar. When Trigger got in the elevator, he saw four undercover police rush the young kid in the building. Trigger knew his story all too well. He saw it every day in the land of poverty.

Once on the fifth floor, he saw his baby mother's door open as always because she grew up out here and everybody loved her. Trigger walked through the clean place, surprised to see nobody was home because he had just spoken to Venessa an hour ago.

He walked to the master bedroom and he saw a father's worst nightmare. His daughter's head was chopped off her body and placed on the bed next to Venessa's body. Trigger cried looking at the bloody gruesome scene, which was like one he had only seen in horror movies.

"You like my work?" Andy asked, sliding out of the closet with a Mack 11 in his hand and blood all over his clothes and hands.

"You feel good?"

"Yeah, I do, Trigger. You crossed the wrong nigga, so now you have to pay the price"

"I trusted you, and this is how you do me, fam? I could have been killed you, but I didn't," Trigger said, trying not to look at his daughter and his baby mother.

"Number one rule to the game: trust no one," Andy said before firing seven rounds into Trigger's temple. "Bitch nigga."

Andy walked out with blood on the bottom of his new Giuseppe sneakers.

***

Manhattan, NY
Weeks later

Paola had been staying at a nice classy hotel in the city, where she had peace and quiet. Her hotel was pimped out with state-of-the-art everything and two master bedrooms with walk-in closets. She needed time to form a plan because shit was a little harder than she expected. Every time she saw Wolf, she had all the chances to kill him, but for some reason, her emotions took over her every time she saw him.

She was taking a long hot shower, trying to clear her thoughts and focus on her mission. When she was done, she stepped out of the shower in the hotel towel with her long hair dripping down her back.

"Took you long enough," Wolf said, sitting on her bed with a gun in his hand, scaring the life out of her.

"Romeo," she stated, wondering how he got past her guards in the next room.

"I killed your soldiers next door, if that's what you was thinking," Wolf said, looking at her body, trying not to be turned on, but she was the baddest bitch he ever saw and she was still his wife.

"Why are you here? To kill me?" she said as if it was a joke. She grabbed her lotion off the table to rub it on her legs and body in front of him.

Wolf watched the way she put lotion on and it looked like a soft porn movie. "Maybe."

"Well, can you at least help me put lotion on my back? You still my husband," she said, handing him the lotion.

Wolf placed his pistol in his back and helped her with the lotion. Feeling her soft skin brought back old memories.

Paola turned around with glossy eyes and stepped on her toes to kiss his lips. She grabbed his dick, pulling his snake out of his pants, and it was on and popping.

Wolf unwrapped her towel and threw her on the bed. He climbed between her legs, entering the warm wet tightness he loved so much. Wolf fucked her hard and rough for hours as she screamed in pleasure and pain.

He showed no remorse even when he saw blood from busting her open too rough. Her yells and screams could be heard for hours.

Chapter 31

Sleepy Hollow, NY

CB got off exit four on his way to check on Bella after a long day with his mother. She spent hours talking about Wolf. CB found it funny that Wolf tried to give her a taste of her own blood. His mother was starting to get on his nerves about this Wolf situation, but he had to listen because every time he did, Rita would start sucking his dick. CB knew it was wrong and nasty, but her head game had him begging her for more. She knew some tricks. He climaxed six times in less than five minutes today and Rita drank all of his milk like a champ, fucking his head up.

CB parked his Ferrari next to Bella's car and went upstairs, hoping Bella was asleep and wasn't in the mood for sex because he was drained in every sense. He walked through the door and placed his keys and phone on the doorway table. He never worried about Bella going through his phone because she wasn't that type of chick. That's why he loved her so much: because she was different.

"Bella, baby," CB said, walking into their room, which was dark, to see Bella under the covers asleep. CB was quiet enough not to wake her as he tippy-toed to her bed.

When he took off his shoes he saw the bed covers fly in the air and a woman jump out with a pistol pointing at him. Paola turned on the light on the lamp to see the look on CB's face, which was priceless.

"CB, nice to meet you."

"Who are the fuck are you, and where is Isabella?"

"Right here," Paola said, walking backwards with her gun still aimed at him. Paola opened the closet door. Bella was hogtied with duct tape around her mouth. Paola grabbed Bella by her hair and dragged her on the carpet, tossing her in the middle of the floor.

Seeing Bella cry in pain did something to CB's soul because he really loved her.

"I'm Paola – Wolf's wife and soon to be his widow after I kill him," she said with no shame.

"What do you want from us? Just let her go please."

"Awwwww, you caught feelings for your brother's leftovers. The thirst is real, papi," Paola said, looking at Bella's puppy dog eyes.

"Take me, but leave her alone."

"I may be able to do that, but I want you to cut her face open the way y'all do it in prison," Paola said, excited.

"What?"

"Cut her face. It's a blade on the dresser. And keep your hands where I can see them. I already took all the weapons you hid around the room."

CB thought she was joking at first, but then he saw how serious the crazy bitch was and he followed her orders. CB had a pistol in his back pocket, but he knew his chances of getting to that were slim because Paola was on his heels. He picked up the blade and looked at Bella's begging eyes, feeling guilty, but he knew it was the only way.

"If I do this, she goes free?"

"Yes. I'm a woman of my word. At least after I kill you, she won't be able to be with another nigga. It's a win-win type of thing," Paola explained.

"You're sick," CB told her.

CB closed his eyes and swung the blade at Bella's face, feeling it slice her cheek wide open. When CB opened his eyes, he saw Bella's right cheek flipped open, bleeding everywhere. Hearing her scream under the tape made him cry. He dropped the blade and hearing Paola put him in a rage.

"Nice one, papi. I'ma keep my word."

Boc! Boc! Boc!

CB caught one bullet to the head and two to the chest. Bella saw the whole scene and was in the *Twilight Zone*.

Paola took the tape off from around Bella's mouth, squatting down to look at the nasty long cut across her face.

"I bet Wolf don't want you after he see you like this. I was riding his dick so good a couple of nights ago that I almost got sidetracked that I was there to kill him," Paola said.

"Just kill me," Bella mumbled through her cries.

"Nope," Paola said, walking out, laughing loud.

***

Brooklyn, NY

Since the beef with the Jamaicans was over, Demon was spending a lot of time in the Brooklyn trenches.

Demon was driving through the mall parking lot to find a parking space. He saw a thick, light-skinned, Spanish chick with big tits walking to a Range with shopping bags. It was two days before Christmas so Demon knew it would be hell trying to find a parking spot because most people last minute shop in New York.

"Excuse me, are you coming out?" Demon asked her, seeing her beautiful smile.

"Yeah, handsome, I got you," she said, looking at his 666 tattoo on his face. "Nice tat."

"Thanks. Nice body."

"Glad you watching it."

"I would love to do more than watch," Demon said, going back and forth with her.

"Maybe we can make that happen. I'm a little horny nowadays."

'I would love to satisfy your needs."

"You and every other man. I like your swag and vibes. What you doing later? Let's grab a bite to eat from a bar and grill spot downtown."

"Cool, just send me the location," Demon said, passing her his phone so she could put her number in it.

When she got inside the candy red Range, Demon stared at her big nice ass bouncing in her jeans.

Romell Tukes

Chapter 32

Downtown Brooklyn
Days later

"Mmmmmm...sssss..." Demon moaned on his back in the hotel's dark room, feeling his dick slide in the back of K Baby's throat. K Baby was the Spanish chick he met at the mall days ago in the parking lot. After speaking for a couple of days, they made plans to go out to eat and hit the hotel for a nightcap to see where shit would go.

After a little foreplay, K Baby wasted no time in pulling out his dick, slobbing on his pipe. "You taste so good, zaddy," she moaned going up and down on his shaft like the pro she was. Saliva was everywhere.

"Suck this dick, you nasty bitch!" Demon yelled, turning her on, making her pick up the pace, forcing her head deeper and deeper until tears came out of her eyes and snot out of her nose. When he erupted in her mouth, she moaned. She swallowed everything while jerking him off, getting him aroused again.

"Fuck me from the back, papi," she said, bending over on the edge of the bed, giving him a full view of her big firm ass.

"Damn," Demon said, grabbing her hips with both hands and slowly putting the tip in, feeling her tight grip. When she started to loosen up, he picked up the pace and started to kill her shit.

"Ooohhh yesss! Oh shit, papi!" she yelled, biting the pillow and gripping the bed sheets because it was too much pain.

Demon couldn't hold himself. Her pussy was so good. He felt a spurt come out of his chest before he shot his load in her. Demon turned her over by her legs and the craziest shit he ever saw in his life happened.

K Baby's leg came off. It was an artificial leg made of plastic. He was at a loss for words as he looked at K Baby, who tossed the bed sheet over her body, embarrassed.

"I'm sorry. I should have had told you," she said sadly, putting her leg back on.

Demon had wondered why she was in such a rush to turn off the lights. "It's okay," Demon said, looking at the cream pouring out of her pretty pussy, which was getting him hard again.

"I think we should take a break for tonight so we can talk. You may need a drink for this," she said, getting up, putting on a robe, and walking out of the room as Demon followed her. "I haven't been all the way honest with you, Demon," she said, calling him by his nickname, which he never gave her

"Please don't tell me. You set me up?" he said, thinking about how his gun was in the room if she was to try anything.

"Not really. When we met, I had some of my people look into you and come to find out you are connected to the man who killed my husband, Mad Max, and my father Jimenez," she said, bringing him a glass of Henny on the rocks.

"So what, you want to poison me?" Demon asked, looking into the glass for any type of foul play.

"I would never. The dick is too good." She laughed. "But I know you work for Andy, who is good friends with Wolf, the man I'm looking for."

"And?"

"I want you and your friend Force to come work for me and build our own empire. I have the drugs, the plug, and the money. We can even move out of the country."

"Just like that? How do I know I can trust you? Because I knew who you were all along, Karol Jimenez. I was just waiting for you to be truthful with me."

"Smart. I like that. So when did you find out?" She took a sip of her drink, crossing her fake legs.

"I was watching Mad Max and you caught my eye. You're beautiful," he said, making her blush.

Karol recently got her fake legs last month and she felt like a new bitch, but she only ever wore jeans to conceal her legs. "So are you with me?"

"Let me speak to Force and see what he thinks. I'll get back to you. But until then, come ride this dick," he said, seeing her get up and ready for another round.

***

Jones Beach
Months later

Winter was finally over and the beaches were wide open again. Paola had a beach towel wrapped around her body as she walked to her Rolls Royce truck with three security guards behind her.

Paola had been more focused on business than war, but she was still putting a plan together to take out Wolf and his little crew. She spoke to her father that morning. He wanted her to come see him this week and she agreed.

Walking through the lot, she always paid close attention to her surroundings, so when she saw the light-skinned dude posted up on his car staring at her and her crew, she got on alert. Not too long after that, shots started to ring out and the light-skinned nigga hit two of her guards, killing them.

Paola had a pistol in her Chanel bag. She pulled it out and went to work, firing at the gunman. Her last guard jumped in front of her gunfire and caught two bullets to the back of his head.

She and the light-skinned nigga were shooting back and forth. Paola took her clip out and dropped it to reload. She popped back up to see the light-skinned dude pulling off in a white pearl Benz E-class sedan.

Paola hopped in her Rolls Royce truck, getting away from the crime scene, trying to figure out who was just trying to end her life. On her way out of the lot, she saw Julie laid back in a Bentley coupe, waving at her.

Paola's blood boiled. She wanted to hop out and air her shit out, but she knew she would have her chance again soon.

Romell Tukes

Chapter 33

Yonkers, NY

Force and Demon were on Elm Street, smoking and drinking with twenty young gangstas posted up, trying to make a couple of dollars to feed their starving stomachs.

"Yo, bro, you just met this bitch. How you know she not lying?"

"Nigga, the bitch knows everything. I know you fuck with Andy, bro, but what is he really doing for us, son? We cop our own drugs and put in our own work out here," Demon stated, speaking the truth.

"I'm not denying that, bro, but you missing the point. We about loyalty, bro. Andy put us on the map. We can't just turn on him."

"We not. We just moving up in the game. If a nigga can't understand that, then he's dead weight to us, boy," Demon stated.

Force kept quiet because he knew where his boy was from. But even if he was to cross sides and do his own thing, a good friendship would be lost.

"Holler at shawty so we can have a real live one on one sit down to make sure our next move is our best move, bro. Facts,"

"Got you," Demon said, smiling.

***

Manhattan, NY
Weeks later

Salma was in her skyrise condo, looking out her terrace into the bright city, thinking about her life and what it had come to. Now that it was nice out again, she had plans to complete her mission. There was only one thing stopping her and she wasn't ready to tell anybody just yet.

Salma had to fly out to Puerto Rico in the morning to meet with a couple of her clients about some coke prices because there was a big drought across the east coast. She had a plan to flood the streets soon and take care of her unfinished business.

***

San Quentin Prison, Cali

Paola was waiting on Ruiz to come out. She hated jail visits. Ever since she was a kid and her mom would bring her up here to see her dad and she always got the chills.

She needed a break from New York so going back home to the west coast was well needed for her. Earlier she went to her mom's and brother's gravesites to visit them.

Wolf had been on her mind a lot lately but she couldn't let her emotions overcome her plans and goals. She knew she could become a victim to her own mission.

Ruiz walked in the small booth, happy to see his baby, knowing she had some good news for him that would make his day.

"Hi baby."

"Hey, Father, you look good."

"Thanks. How are things in New York? I got all your letters? You have the best army behind you, baby. They will protect you as if you was me."

"They're useless for what I'm up against, Father. It's bad, I have so many people coming at me that I can't tell who is who."

"I understand. But cut the head off and the body will fall"

"This is the type of head that's hard to detach," she said, referring to her husband.

"You still love him. I see it in your eyes"

"I do, but that doesn't make a difference. I know what needs to be done."

"Oh, you do? So why are you still dealing with Wolf's mother Rita? I told you she will end up crossing you and leaving you in some ditch. Don't be stupid." Ruiz tried to hurt her feelings, but she laughed.

"My time is up." Paola got up to leave, causing him to get upset.

"I'll have your head, just like the rest of them!" Ruiz yelled at her back.

***

Bronx, NY

Force was in his new crib watching Mia dance on the stripper pole he had in the middle of the floor.

Mia was wearing a two-piece lingerie set and her body was crazy. Force had never seen an ass so big in his life and he was ready to fuck. Old school slow jams played in the background, setting the mood.

Mia grabbed the pole, bending over, grabbing her ankles, bouncing her ass and making it clap everywhere.   Force   saw her phat pussy and the gap between her thighs and couldn't wait till he got a taste of her love box.

"You ready?" she said, slow walking towards him sexually in her high heels.

"Hell yeah," Force said in his silk boxers, smiling like a Santa who stole Christmas.

"Let me put the cuffs on you so when I suck your big dick you can stay in place, papi," Mia said, placing the real cuffs on his hands.

"Damn, where you get these?"

"Shhhh," she said, kissing his lips, rubbing her big titties over his face. She placed a scarf between the middle of the chain of the cuffs and tied it to the headboard rail.

"You on some freaky 50 Shades of Grey shit up in here," Force said, looking around the dark room.

"I'ma go grab some toys out the bathroom," she said, leaving the room, pulling her G-string out of her ass.

Force was horny and pumped up. He looked around the room and saw a big photo of Mia with the name Melissa above it. He thought of where he had recently heard that name from and then it hit him: Spanish Harlem. The name Melissa was Flaco's sister. He heard she was bad with a lot of money. Force connected the dots. He tried to snatch the scarf off the rail and after the sixth try, he was loose. Force's clothes and gun were down the hall in the other room. He lifted the window latch and pulled it up. The ground was a little jump down. Force still had cuffs on. Once on the ground, he took off.

Mia fired shots from a Draco at him from the window as he got away.

Chapter 34

Newburgh, NY

"You should have seen the look on that bitch's face," Julie told Spice, lying under the covers hot and sticky after an hour of hot sex. The couple had been fucking like two wild jungle animals in heat.

"I almost had that bitch," Spice said, mad that his gun had jammed on him while shooting at Paola.

"Next time, baby," Julie said, rubbing his six pack.

"She was a bad little bitch, you can't lie."

"What?" Julie said, lifting her head

"You know what I mean."

"No, I don't," Julie said, rolling her eyes, getting an attitude.

"Anyway, what you got planned for today?" Spice asked, changing the subject.

"I don't know yet," she said, getting out of the bed to go take a shower. Spice admired her body and beauty. He brought her through the hood yesterday and everybody had their tongues out.

Spice hadn't spoken to Andy. Spice had got a new number for that reason. Spice felt like a traitor, but he was starting to fall in love with Julie. He loved everything about her, especially her bomb-ass pussy.

***

Manhattan, NY
Months later

Salma called Wolf and asked him to come over so they could talk, which made Wolf overthink because he hadn't seen her in over a year.

Wolf had been laying low. He went underground for a while to clear his head so he could regroup because everything was happening so fast in his life. He thought about the last time he fucked Salma and he couldn't deny the fact that she had some good pussy.

Wolf took the elevator to her floor dressed in his Dolce and Gabbana outfit.

Salma opened the door, happy to see him.

"Hey you. Wow, you grew a beard?" she said, leaning in to kiss him but he dodged it. "It's like that?" she said, upset.

"Nah. I'd just rather not get affectionate. You may become an enemy!"

"You can't be serious? Well, if that's how you feel, fuck you! But let me show you something," she said, walking down the hallway of her condo in a mesh Louis Vuitton slip dress and heels.

Wolf saw her ass wobble and shake with every strut, showing she had on no panties, causing him to lust, but he had to control himself. Salma was looking good tonight with her hair in a ponytail and just enough makeup on to bring out her features.

When they walked into a little kids' room which had a carriage and bed for infants in the middle of the room, he was lost.

"I never knew you had a kid. That's what's up. And he's cute," Wolf said, looking at the handsome light-skinned baby dressed in Gucci pajamas.

"How dumb can you be, Wolf? He's your son. I had him a couple of months ago," she said, shaking her head.

"Me?" Wolf said, thinking it was some type of trick or game.

"I did a DNA test. I had my people get a glass you used while we were at a restaurant a while back. That's how I collected your DNA and sent it off to be tested. The test came back as positive," said Salma, pulling up the results on her phone.

"Why didn't you tell me before?" he asked.

"I wasn't ready, and I was not having an abortion, so I took care of my business. Let me make this clear: I don't need you for nothing. I can take care of my own. I'm a strong Puerto Rican woman," she said with glossy eyes.

Wolf walked up to her and kissed her lips, wiping her warm tears from under her eyes. "I'm here with you. I'll never leave my child for dead. I'm not a loser or a deadbeat."

"I hope not."

"What did you name him?"

"Randell Aguilera, your middle name," she replied. She showed him the results on her screen.

Wolf's face lit up. He was now a father. He was overwhelmed. He hugged Salma tightly.

"Damn, nigga, you going to kill me?" she said, happy about his reaction.

"Can I go see him again?"

"He's your child, but if you wake him, you will be feeding him and putting him back to bed. It's 11 p.m. He normally wakes up soon." She watched Wolf walk to his son's room and it made her cry hard.

Wolf spent the night at Salma's crib. They made love all night and talked about all the worrying they were up against. Salma told him about her plan she had in motion for Ruiz and Wolf loved it.

***

San Quentin Prison, Cali

Ruiz had just gotten done praying as lunch came through the bottom of his door. Today was chicken, potatoes, carrots, and applesauce, Ruiz's favorite. Ruiz dug into the applesauce with his plastic spoon. He was very upset about Paola not following his orders because Wolf was supposed to have been dead.

He knew his daughter was smart, but he also knew females had strong emotions, especially her.

Ruiz felt his heart rate speed up and he couldn't breathe. He rushed to the emergency button near his sink, pushing it five times before he fell out and started to go in shock. The guards came to his cell ten minutes later to see he was laid out on the ground with foam pouring out of his mouth, dead.

Romell Tukes

Chapter 35

Lower East Side, NY

Rita was driving in her Benz G-wagon truck, all-black with black rims and tints. Paola had called her and told her she was finally ready for her. Rita was excited because she was getting low on bricks and business was jumping.

Since CB's death, she had been rebuilding her army and finding new workers, which was the easy part. But replacing a son was hard. Even though Rita killed her own daughter and tried to have both Wolf and Black killed, Rita still believed in family business morals. She couldn't bring herself to shed a tear when she buried CB at a private ceremony because he picked a street life, so he knew the outcome, which was jail or death and he got a taste of both.

With so many people coming at her head, she didn't know who killed CB, nor did she really care. If they came her way next, she was prepared.

Paola asked her to come alone for some reason and Rita agreed. She liked Paola. She was about her business. There was a funny vibe she would get from her at times but she did her best not to overlook things, which seemed to be her life story.

She saw Paola at the entrance of the gate leaning on a Rolls Royce truck. Paola wore a white mink coat, blending in with the small snowfall. Rita saw the abandoned factories in the background, wondering why she would want to meet down here on the Hudson River side.

"Hey."

"What's up, Paola? It's a little cold out here. Let's go in my truck. I got the heat on," Rita said, putting her Miu Miu hoodie over her head.

"This won't take long," Paola said in a scary tone, pulling out a FN handgun with 223 bullets.

"What's going on?" Rita said with her hands in the air.

"Bitch, let's not play dumb. You know who I am and I know who you are. Like you really thought I was going to let you kill me, bitch?" Paola asked her a trick question.

"I was going to kill you after I got this shipment, but I guess greed beat me to my death today. I know Ruiz would be proud of you if he hadn't been poisoned."

"Life sucks sometimes, you know."

"So I guess this is the part where I have to beg for my life or you ask me a dumb-ass questions before you kill me?" Rita asked.

"No, I just plan to kill you," Paola replied in a nonchalant tone.

Paola shot Rita in the face while the snow starting coming down hard. Paola took one last look at Rita before climbing into her new Rolls Royce truck.

Paola knew Rita was Wolf's mom and she would sooner or later cross her, so today she had her on deadline. Her next mission was finding out who killed her father. She had gotten a call from her cousin Audrey today letting her know she was in New York and wanted to meet with her sometime this week.

***

Auburn Maximum Security Prison
Days later

OG Chuck hadn't left his cell all day since the prison chaplain told him his son and baby mother were found dead a while back. OG wished he spent more time with CB as a son to build that father and son bond. Losing his daughter Victoria and now a second son took everything out of him. He was stuck doing life in a prison cell with no chance of parole or anything, so he felt hopeless.

OG knew Rita had something to do with all of this mayhem. He didn't care that she got killed because she was a grimy bitch in his book and had gotten everything she had coming to her.

Tears filled his eyes as he laid on his small hard bunk, staring at his blue ceiling, hearing someone upstairs jumping up and down like they had lost their mind.

***

Yonkers, NY

Andy and Wolf were standing and talking outside the Empire Casino. They both spent hours inside gambling only to lose 150K apiece, but luckily it was pocket change for them both. Wolf had just gotten done speeding Andy up on everything that had been going on with CB and Rita and his newborn with his dad's girlfriend.

"Damn, bro, I'm sorry to hear about your mom. I know she was out to get you, but that's still your mother," Andy said, puffing on Newport cigarettes.

"Yeah, but to be real, I don't feel shit. I think any love I had for her was washed away when she was trying to kill me," Wolf said seriously.

"Oh, I forgot. I got something for you," Andy said, going inside his Yukon truck to grab a piece of paper.

"What's this?" Wolf said, looking at the Sleepy Hollow address on a small yellow paper.

"I followed Paola there when she killed your brother. I been on her heels. That bitch crazy. How could you marry something like that?"

"I didn't know she was G.I. Jane," Wolf said, making Andy laugh as a black Bentley pulled into the lot.

"Oh, this is my girl, the one I was telling you about, bro. She is bad and gangsta," Andy said, opening the driver's side door for Maryanna, who hopped out in a Givenchy peacoat and scarf.

"Aunty!" Wolf shouted, seeing her face, hoping he was tripping. Andy looked at Wolf like he was bugging out.

"Romeo, nice to see you. It's been a while. I'm very impressed by your work," Maryanna said, kissing his cheek.

"You his aunt?" Andy asked, confused.

"Yes. I know him as Romeo, not Wolf. Can you give us a minute, baby? I need to talk to Romeo alone," Maryanna said in her sweet voice.

"You fucking my aunt? Oh, payback is a bitch," Wolf said, smiling.

Andy laughed and got in the Bentley, letting them talk for over an hour in private.

Chapter 36

Brooklyn, NY

Karol was inside her Caribbean restaurant full of gangstas. Karol was street smart and book smart just like her father but because she was handicapped, people looked past everything else.

Marrying Mad Max was the worst mistake of her life, but she had felt no one else would marry her because of her disability.

Being with a man like Mad Max who had a wealthy family supplying him endless amounts of drugs put her in a win-win position. Karol came up with her own plan after a while. She just needed the right crew to come along and have the balls to take Mad Max to war. When Andy killed Zion, the brother of Mad Max, she knew it was time to put her plan into slow motion.

Everything worked out perfectly. She only had one problem: Mad Max's family in Jamaica wanted answers for his death. Mad Max's parents were drug lords and household names in Jamaica, and Karol needed a crew to go silence them and bring back the millions of dollars' worth of drugs in Mad Max's family home in Kingston, Jamaica.

Mad Max always told her about a tunnel in his parents house filled with drugs. She needed a crew to go there and bring back the goodies for her. The crew she had in mind just pulled up outside.

***

Force and Demon walked into the restaurant, looking around to see evil dread heads.

"What the fuck is this?" Force said loud enough so the whole room could hear him.

"It's okay. These men are here to protect me."

"And who the fuck are you?" Force asked.

"Bro, chill," Demon said, seeing Karol's face.

"I know how this may look, but I want you both to come help me build this empire," she said.

"Why us?" Force asked.

"Because you two together are worth more than you're settling for," Karol said.

"So you can give us better?" Force said

"Yes," she replied.

"Well, shoot," Demon said, all ears.

"Mad Max's parents were supplying him drugs and the run of Jamaica. They started the Shower Posse and are Jamaica's main suppliers. They have a mansion with a tunnel filled with bricks and if you two can find a way to go get the keys, we can split it 50/50 and take over the Brooklyn and Yonkers streets. I have an army that will assist you and follow your lead," she said, looking at them both

"So you want us to risk our life for 50/50?" Demon now spoke up

"Baby, it's fair. We can work as a team instead of being greedy. Think of all the money we will see off this. I'm talking tons."

"How do you know all of this? And how do we know you not bullshitting us?" Force asked the big question Demon wasn't asking. Demon had to go home to Karol and he wanted some head later, so he kept his mouth shut.

"I saw it myself on me and Mad Max's honeymoon to his parents' home in Jamaica. He sneaked me into his parents' room and moved the dresser. It's tall like a china cabinet. There was a small door with a punch-in code I remember, which was his birthday. Then we took an elevator to an underground tunnel. That's when I saw it all," she said, lying, telling them pieces of what Mad Max used to tell her, but adding in her own mix.

"I don't believe you, because why would you want to split everything 50/50 when you can send your goons down there and have it all to yourself?" Force stated, now making Demon looking at her funny.

"I need your skills, point blank. My men are average shooters. You two are advanced shooters."

"Let us sleep on it and we will get back at you," Force said, getting up to leave. Demon was still sitting playing footsies with Karol. "Come on."

Demon got up and kissed her juicy soft lips, telling her he would see her later.

***

Sleepy Hollow, NY

Bella was packing up the last little bit of her clothes so she could catch her flight to Atlanta where she could start over, because New York was taking a toll on her. Last night she almost found herself in a dope house about to cop heroin, but luckily nobody answered the door.

Ever since she lost CB, her life had shattered into pieces again. The news of CB and Wolf being brothers was crazy to her. She felt nasty and as if CB used her.

The scar across her face was healing, but it was big and deep. She hated CB for doing that to her, but he did save her life and risked his own for her to live. But now she had a scar on her face to remember Paola and CB every time she looked in the mirror.

She had just placed tape on her last box when she heard the doorbell ring. The movers were supposed to arrive five minutes ago to pack her belongings in a U-Haul truck and drive it to Atlanta to a nice apartment.

"You're late. I have to——" Bella paused when she saw Wolf standing there with a gun in his hand.

"Go sit," Wolf said, forcing her into the crib, closing the door behind him.

"Romeo, why are you doing this?" she screamed, crying.

"Save the tears, bitch. Why did you sell me out to your father when I first met you? And don't lie. Salma told me everything."

"I know my dad used strong men, but I didn't know he was going to have your sister killed, and I didn't know someone paid him to kill you. I thought he was going to blackmail you somehow and pay you to kill. I was trying to help you. I saw murder in your eyes when I first saw you. My aunty Salma is just like my father."

"So are you, Bella."

"Romeo, please, I'm sorry."

Boom! Boom! Boom! Boom!

The bullets tore through her head, knocking her body on the floor. Wolf walked out of the apartment hurting because he had love for Bella, but once he found out how she crossed him, the love was gone.

Chapter 37

Upper Westside, NY

Salma and Wolf were leaving the hotel room. They spent the weekend making love and getting to know each other better. They were both horny and needed an emotional escape, so they agreed to meet up. They knew now they had no choice but to be in each other's lives to raise a son, and the sexual feelings were still there. After coming to an agreement that they would have sex with no strings attached, everything seemed easier to cope with.

"What do you have planned for the night?" Salma asked in the elevator, fixing her hair in the glass mirror.

"I gotta go to New Jersey to handle some shit, but I'ma come back to spend some time with my son," Wolf said, walking through the lobby.

"You better."

Outside, it was dark. Out of the corner of Salma's eye, she saw a group of masked men coming from behind cars.

"Wolf!" Salma yelled.

Wolf was already on point. He saw the play. When he stepped outside, he saw shadows lurking. Wolf spun around, firing first, and Salma followed his lead, firing her pistol with the thirty round clip towards another group of men.

Salma saw Paola firing shots towards them.

"Bitch!" Salma shouted, ducking, seeing the evil in her eyes like a woman gone insane. Wolf saw Paola too and didn't hesitate to shoot in her direction, hitting three of her guards.

"Get in the car," Wolf told Salma while shooting in every direction the shooters were coming from.

Salma hit the push to start button on the Audi once she got inside. "Get in!" she yelled at Wolf, who had just taken a bullet to the thigh from Paola.

"Ahhhhhhh!" Wolf yelled, feeling the burn but still firing, hitting two more of Paola's goons with head shots before climbing in the back seat of the Audi. When he was inside, Salma pulled off at top speed.

"This bitch just shot me!" Wolf yelled, holding on to his thigh, bleeding in her back seat.

"I know someone in Washington Heights who will fix you up. Stop crying. It's a turn off."

"You get shot then let me tell you that!" he screamed at her.

"Calm down, angry bird," she said trying to lighten up the mood.

Twenty minutes later, Salma brought Wolf to a nurse she had known for years from Brazil. The old lady had a hospital room in her basement where she worked on civilians and people with no green cards. It didn't take long for the bullet to come out and for Wolf to get patched up.

*****

Yonkers, NY

Force was chilling with Audrey inside of one of his stash spots.

"I think I'ma take her up on her offer. What you think?" Force asked while placing money into two counting machines on the living room table.

"I'll come to Jamaica with you if you want, because this story sounds too fishy, baby," Audrey said, walking over to Force in her booty shorts.

"Nah, it's believable, but I'ma still give it some time before I make up my mind. She wants to meet again to talk," Force said as Audrey sat on his lap.

"I want to come with you next time because I don't trust this bitch," she said, feeling his hand rub all over her smooth thighs.

"I got it, baby, just relax," Force said, kissing her lips, sliding his finger into her wet pussy.

"Mmmmmm, yesss," she said, standing up, taking off her tight shorts and undressing him.

The two started having rough sex right on the table, almost breaking the legs.

***

Liberty, NY

Judge Belanger had been a judge in Brooklyn for over twenty years. He was an elderly white man with a wife and two grown children. He lived upstate New York in a nice house with his wife Jamie. His son Jacob was in town for the week with his wife Winney coming up from Florida to celebrate his father's birthday.

"Mom, what you cooking?" Jacob entered the kitchen to see Jamie and Winney cooking a big Italian meal. Their family was Italian and they kept their family traditions.

"Pasta, your father's favorite. And your lovely wife is baking the cake and cupcakes," his mom stated, whipping the tomato sauce with her secret recipe inside.

The doorbell rang and Jacob left the kitchen to answer it because his father was in the basement watching a football game in his den. Jacob opened the door to see a sexy Latino woman standing there with a bright smile.

"Excuse me, I just moved around the neighborhood and I need——"

Psst! Psst! Psst!

Maryanna shot him three times in the head and watched his body drop as she walked into the house. She heard voices coming from the kitchen, so she made her way inside the kitchen to see an old lady cooking and singing to herself. When Jamie turned around, she was startled after seeing the handgun with the silencer attached to it.

Psst! Psst! Psst! Psst!

Bullets knocked the wind out of her chest as she fell into the kitchen cabinets.

Maryanna walked around the house looking for the judge, but she didn't see him upstairs or anywhere else. She saw a door leading into the basement. Maryanna heard a TV playing. She took her time creeping downstairs, trying not to make any noise on the wooden stairs. Downstairs, she saw an old pool table, a bar, and a bunch of old dusty boxes. Making her way deeper into the basement, she saw a living room area where a white chick's titties were bouncing up and down.

Judge Belanger was fucking the shit out of his son's wife. She was riding his, dick making her go crazy

"Ummm, ohhhh yesss, fuck me!" Winney screamed, hoping her husband didn't hear her upstairs.

Judge Belanger and Winney had been having an affair for over ten years. Winney used to work under him before she met his son. She was twenty-five years younger than him but she loved his dick game and always came back for more.

Psst! Psst!

Winney's body rolled off Judge Belanger onto the floor after catching two shots in her face.

Judge Belanger had the fear of God on his face before Maryanna emptied the clip into his head.

Chapter 38

Bronx, NY

Audrey and Paola were having dinner at a small Spanish restaurant, catching up on old times. Audrey was Cruz's daughter, so she and Paola spent many birthdays together as kids, but when Audrey went into the Navy, they lost contact.

"You look the same as you did as a kid," Paola told her cousin.

"You do too. Thanks for coming out. This is so long past due. It seems we have the same motive, because Sousa's wife killed my father along with some guy named Wolf."

Hearing Wolf's name always brought goosebumps to Paola's body. "I believe you can be very useful, and vice versa. I do have a location on Julie. I've been watching her very close. She is in Newbury with a drug dealer named Spice," Paola stated

"Damn, you're on point. I'ma make a trip up there soon, then I want to hunt for Wolf. I'ma need some help with him," Audrey stated, looking at Paola's wedding ring, unaware she was married.

"I got you. I'ma look into him also," Paola promised her.

"Thanks. Mmmm, how come I was never invited to the wedding?"

"The what?"

"The wedding. You're married, right?" Audrey said, looking at the big rock on her finger.

"Ohhh, no, I just wear this to keep guys away from me. You know how these New York dudes are. They will chase you down for blocks trying to spit game."

Audrey agreed because before she walked into the restaurant, a dude followed her for a block trying to bag her even after she told him she was taken. "I understand. I have to meet my boyfriend. Call me later with the Newbury info, Paola. Thanks for everything."

Audrey got up to leave, feeling Paola stare a hole in her back. It was nice to see her favorite cousin, but her vibes were off. Audrey could tell Paola's mind was elsewhere.

If Paola snaked her, Audrey had already made a promise to herself to kill Paola where she stood, family or not. Audrey was playing by her own rules on her own mission.

There was something about Paola's attitude that made her think she had her own agenda. Audrey knew it was a cold game and nobody could be trusted.

***

Manhattan, NY

Salma played with her son on the floor, helping him crawl all over the place, strengthening his legs.

Wolf had just left her crib after spending time with his son. They had something good going, and she hoped it lasted forever, but the life they both lived made it hard to keep promises.

Motherhood was beautiful. She didn't mind the breastfeeding, waking up at all hours of the night, or changing diapers when needed.

Growing up, Salma's mother was a strong independent Puerto Rican woman who raised her to be the same and never depend on a man for nothing.

Salma had her crew running all of her drug operations in New York and Puerto Rico because she needed time for her newborn. She also wanted to kill Paola for the little move she tried to put on a few weeks ago outside the hotel.

Wolf admitted to Salma that he recently had sexual interactions with Paola and she told him she didn't care, but deep down, she really did.

With nothing but time on her hands, all she had been doing was planning and plotting.

***

Newburgh, NY
Weeks later

Spice had just left his crib. He was on his way out of town to Boston where he had a crew moving weight for him, thanks to Julie blessing him with close to four hundred pounds of weed from Cali and a hundred bricks of pure Colombian coke. Julie was in Cali for the weekend handling some business transactions. Spice was glad Julie had kept her word because now he had Newbury, Albany, Rochester, and Boston under his wings. He had crews in each city now making him rich. He still felt bad for turning on Andy, but the little ten to thirty keys he was getting from him was a day of work now.

Spice pulled his Ferrari into the gas station to get gas before he headed up to Boston to check on his Cabo Verdean crew. A black Cadillac CTS parked across from him and a sexy Spanish bitch jumped out, catching his attention. Spice loved Latina women. He was hooked since meeting Julie. He had been trying to get her to open up about a future threesome, but she wasn't having it at all.

Spice followed the woman into the store to pay for his gas. The woman was paying for her gas also and she was in front of him, giving him a clear look at her nice round ass - not too much; just perfect. When she turned around to leave, she almost knocked him over, unaware someone was so close behind her.

"Excuse me," she said, making eye contact with him, giving him a light smile.

"You good, ma," Spice said, inhaling her strong Chloe perfume scent.

After paying for gas, Spice rushed outside to catch a last glimpse of the mystery woman, but she was gone. Spice didn't even see her pump her gas, but he thought nothing of it.

While pumping his gas, he answered a phone call from his cousin. Spice got done and got in his Ferrari, but before he started the foreign car, bullets shattered his windows and eight entered his skull.

Audrey was parked across the street from the gas station in the Cadillac with her military assault rifle out the window.

"Gotcha," she said to herself as the store clerk ran outside with his shotgun to see what happened.

***

Two days later
New York, JFK Airport

Julie had just landed back in New York from Cali, where she had to meet with two new clients and bust down her shipment that came from Colombia. Spice was going to be happy when she told him the good news about the three hundred keys she had for him. Her mind was really focused on taking over New York and Spice was going to help her. That's why he was around. But the beef was starting to get old.

Julie had been calling Spice's phone for two days, only to get his voicemail. She prayed he was okay. She walked through the airport and stopped at a bar to grab a drink real quick.

"Two shots of Patron please," she asked the young white handsome bartender.

Sitting down, she just so happened to look above the liquor shelves to see a flat screen TV. But it wasn't the TV that got her full attention. It was the person on the screen.

It was a picture of Spice. The news reporter was explaining how a kingpin was found murdered in his car at a Newburgh gas station and that the killer was on the loose.

Julie knew it was time to get the fuck out of New York, so she booked a flight to Miami, where she had a condo on South Beach.

Chapter 39

Bronx, NY

Andy had been laying low for the past couple of months. He even shut down his drug operation until he figured shit out, but it seemed everything was coming to light. He was tailing the Cadillac CTS through the busy Fordham area of the BX. The woman he had been following...he had no clue who she was. All he knew was she killed Spice, and she was in some type of relationship with his worker Force. Andy hadn't spoken to Force or Spice in months, so he didn't know what was going on. He was in Newburgh stalking Spice to see why he switched up and changed numbers. He thought he was snitching because the Feds hit his Peekskill spot. Spice and Force were the only ones who know about those areas, so he wanted to see if his gut feeling was on point. Now he was wanted by the Feds. Andy was at the top of the twenty-two man indictment.

Seeing his childhood friend get killed hurt him deeply. It was so quick and smooth that he didn't even see it coming. Since that day, he had been tailing the black Cadillac, trying to figure out who she was.

Mia was nowhere to be found. He swore if he ever saw her, he would torture her. Andy couldn't believe Mia was Flaco's brother and she was lining him up the whole time. He was mad at himself for not putting two and two together, especially after the shootout in Spanish Harlem. Mia set the whole scene up when he was coming to get her from work at the salon. Her goons were supposed to shoot up his car and kill him in the car, but luckily he got out of the car at the corner store where they were awaiting him. With Mia's real name being Melissa, he knew he would have never been able to figure that out if it wasn't for the photo of her in the bedroom of her crib.

Andy saw the black Cadillac pull over at the curb of a rundown apartment building. He watched the slim sexy Spanish chick walk into an alley, heading to the back of the building, looking over her shoulder.

It was now or never, so Andy got out with his Conehead hoodie on, crossing the street, making his way to the dirty alley full of big rats running back and forth looking for anything to eat.

***

Audrey approached the man dressed in an army uniform. He was standing there waiting on his wife, whom he married in the army.

"Baby, I miss you so much," Branden said, hugging Audrey tightly and kissing her lips.

"I miss you too," she replied, looking into his hazel eyes.

Branden was from New Jersey. He was always overseas on tours on the frontline, fighting for America. When they met in basic training, it was love at first sight. He was African-American, tall, handsome, lean and muscular, with brown skin, hazel eyes, a goatee, and a low haircut.

Audrey didn't tell Branden her real reason for being in New York, but he never questioned her. He was just happy to finally see her. It'd been almost two years and he wanted to make love to her.

"You ready to go upstairs? It's not the best place, but I found the room on Craigslist." Branden grabbed her hand to go in the building through the back because he was AWOL right now from the Marines. Branden had run away from his VA Fort Lee base to come see Audrey. He missed her that much.

"Hold on," Andy said, popping out from around the corner with a gun in his hand.

"We——"

Andy shot Branden in the neck, dropping him to the ground. Audrey went down with him in tears because she really loved Branden. He had her heart and had taken her V-card. He was special to her.

"More like it. Stand the fuck up, bitch!" Andy said, but she was still holding on to Branden, even after he took his last breath. "You a tough bitch, I see. Don't make me ask you again," Andy demanded and she listened, slowly raising up.

"I should have been killed you," she stated with hatred in her eyes.

"Who are you?"

"I'm here to kill Wolf and you, but looks like it's a change of plans," she said, raising her eyebrows. "You damn right. You thought I was slacking? I'm about that life, shawty. You should have done your research. It's sad because you a bad little bitch. I bet you would have been a good fuck."

"I guess we will never know now, will we?" she said, seeing if she could seduce her way out of this.

"Your pussy probably look nasty and smell like horse shit."

"Find out. I bet I will turn you out."

"Maybe another day."

Boc! Boc! Boc!

Andy made sure she was dead before he turned around to leave. He was unaware someone was behind him. A metal pipe slammed into his forehead, knocking him clean out.

***

Queens, NY

Andy woke up to dogs barking around him, chained to large pipes, trying to get to him. He was in the middle of a small circle in a large basement of some type.

"Shhhh," a female voice whispered, coming out of a dark area dressed in a black satin Gucci strapless dress with six inch heels on. "Good dogs," Karol said, approaching Andy. The dogs didn't make a sound. She looked down at Andy's hands and ankles in zip ties so tight his hands and ankles were swollen.

"What the fuck is going on? I'm sick of seeing you grimy Spanish bitches!" Andy shouted, still bleeding from his forehead.

"Do you like dogs, Andy?"

"What?"

"I said do you like dogs, Andy?" Karol said, petting her bulldog master then her blue nose pitbull. Karol loved dogs so much she bred them and kept them all over the city in seven location because she had over two hundred.

"I do. I'm from Yonkers."

"The home of DMX. He's a dog lover just like me, Andy. When I tell my dogs to kill, they kill. When I tell them to chill, they chill. Where my dogs at?" she shouted and all the dogs started barking uncontrollably. There were seventy dogs in the basement, most in cages in the far back.

"Shhhhh, my children. When I was growing up, I had no friends because I was in a wheelchair, but dogs treated me with love and care - unlike people," Karol said,

"What the fuck does this have to do with me?"

"Shut the fuck up and listen, asshole. Dogs eat dogs' blood and you're a dog just like me, so with it being a dog eat dog world, I'll let you pick the pit bulls or the bulldogs."

"Bitch, fuck you. Who helped you put this plan together?"

"Your boys Force and Demon are the ones who snatched you up for me, but they had to catch a flight to Jamaica, so they couldn't be here to see this," Karol said while walking towards the back.

Andy was watching her every move, but when she came back with four of the biggest pitbulls she had, he was scared shitless. All four pits were over a hundred pounds each. She let the pits attack Andy and it only took ten minutes for them to crush his skull and kill him, leaving a pool of blood as Karol enjoyed the show.

Chapter 40

Miami, FL

Wolf was in Miami on a small vacation and on business. Julie asked him to come down to Miami to talk business because she wanted him on her team while she took over Miami, but she needed a solid army. The Cubans and Haitians controlled Miami's drug trade, so she knew there would be a lot of blood shed if she was to step on their toes. Wolf told Julie he would consider it, but he had a little going on at the moment and he had a son to raise now, he explained to her.

He was in a bar and lounge spot, drinking Henny by the boatload. Wolf wasn't a drinker so he was feeling fucked up, but he wasn't pissy drunk. There were a lot of beautiful women in the lounge, but Wolf wasn't looking for love. He just needed to release some stress. A couple of women approached him, but he wasn't in the mood for small talk if a bitch wasn't trying to fuck. Wolf didn't entertain conversation.

When it hit 1:00 a.m., Wolf left the lounge and walked up the block stumbling. The hotel he was staying at was up the street from the Season One hotel. In the front, he threw up in a flower pot in front of the hotel's sliding doors.

A beautiful woman with a cigarette in her mouth saw Wolf vomiting his heart out and went to help him. When she saw his big face busted down Rolex watch and two heavy diamond GIA necklaces, she thought he was a rapper or somebody major.

"Let it out, sir," she said, patting his back, helping him let it all out. She had many drunk nights, so she knew how it felt.

"Thanks," Wolf said, wiping his mouth.

"Come upstairs to my room. I will make you some coffee," she said, helping him up.

Wolf looked at her body busting out of her tight dress. Her ass was big. He knew it could hold up a Henny bottle.

Once upstairs in the room, Wolf crashed on her couch. He saw female clothes and shoes everywhere.

"Here you go," she said, handing him a fresh cup of Maxwell House coffee.

"Thanks once again," he said, drinking it slowly because it was hot.

"Sure. What's your name?" she asked, sitting next to him, placing her long hair in a ponytail as he eyed her meaty thighs.

"Romeo."

"Nice. You must be down here partying"

"Yeah, I guess you can say that. How about yourself?"

"Same thing. Looking for a little fun," she added, seeing the way he eyed her sexually

"You're sexy," Wolf said, not holding back

"You are too." There was a pause until she got up and walked to her room.

Wolf was no dummy. He knew it was litty. Wolf took off his Balmain outfit as she slid out of her dress, amazed by her curves and big ass with a small waist. She bent over and Wolf got behind her. His dick was so hard it felt like it was going to break any second.

"Ummmm," she moaned, feeling him enter her.

Wolf sobered up upon feeling how tight she was. He spread her wide ass cheeks and went in and out at a good pace, feeling her cream coat the tip of his dick. Wolf closed his eyes, biting his lip, going deeper in her walls, ripping her open

"Uhhhh!" she yelled adjusting to his dick, thrusting her big ass back on his dick.

Wolf slapped her ass a couple of times while she started clapping her ass on his dick, doing tricks, trying to wear him out, working her hips in a rotation.

"I'm cumming on your dick," she moaned and he started to fuck her harder until she climaxed back to back.

When Wolf felt himself about to cum, he pulled out and nutted on her ass, which was putting Buffy Da Body and Pinky to shame.

"Wow. Let's go take a shower so I can show you how good I deep throat underwater," she said, ready to put in some more work.

"Okay. I'ma make another drink."

"A'ight," she said, walking to the private walk-in bathroom connected to the bedroom.

Wolf made himself another drink, ready to fuck her brains out because her pussy was top five. He loved Miami already. Wolf went back in the room and saw her purse, peeking through it real quick before going into the bathroom. When Wolf opened the shower doors, she was playing with her pussy as the shower head water shot at it.

"You think you had me," Wolf said, pointing his Glock 9mm pistol at her.

"What? I don't get it, papi, what's wrong?" she asked, scared.

"You really don't know who I am?" he asked, seeing the look on her face.

"No."

"I'm Wolf."

When he said that name, her face said it all. She wanted to attack him. "Wow, it's a small world. I never saw your face. If I knew it was you, I would have killed you outside," Melissa, a.k.a. Mia, said, standing under the shower in tears because she knew it was over.

"I would let you live, but you would end up killing me. Or we can call this a truce and we can finish what we started because as you see, you're a turn on," he said, looking at his hard-on.

"I will kill you, Wolf, sooner or later, papi, so you have your chance, sexy," she said, wiping her tears.

"A'ight, thanks for your honesty, but I'll take my chances."

Wolf stepped in the shower, kissing her soft lips. She was horny as hell. She wrapped her legs around his waist and Wolf fucked her roughly on the shower wall.

"Ohhhh yessss, Wolf, I love you. Ohhh!" she screamed, feeling Wolf kill her pussy.

Wolf heard what she said but ignored it while fucking her so good he didn't even feel himself nut three times in her wetness.

After two hours of lovemaking, Wolf left the room, leaving her to sleep peacefully with a note under her pillow telling her how special she was and how he would see her again one day.

***

Manhattan, NY

Salma took her son on a stroll in the early morning on the boardwalk of the Hudson River, where joggers normally ran every morning. Salma took a seat on the blue benches to watch the water and boats sailing out. She was waiting on Wolf to come back from Miami so she could tell him she was ready to get out of the game and move to London.   She wanted him to come with her, but she wouldn't force him. That wasn't her style. She wanted a regular life. She had been in the game too long. She gave her empire to her cousin in PR and she had enough money to last six lifetimes.

"Nice view, ain't it?" a voice said before Salma felt a gun barrel to the back of her head.

"I fear nothing," Salma mumbled.

"We all fear something."

Paola blew her head off and then shot the baby three times in his carriage while he was asleep.

Chapter 41

Kingston, Jamaica
Months later

Force and Demon both wore fake dreads with Rasta hats, driving in a blue Land Rover through the "yard", which was Kingston's nickname

"You ready for this?" Force asked Demon, who had an AR-15 in his lap.

"Ready is an understatement, bro."

"Okay," Force said, seeing eight black SUVs pass them, coming from where they were heading up a big hill into a small tropical forest where the mansion was.

"Bro, that had to be them. That's great. Now we can be in and out," Force said, happy to see the trucks in his rearview. It meant less goons he had to worry about trying to kill him.

"Facts. This should be too easy, bro," Demon said, now at the beautiful stone glass mansion which was 27, 419 square foot with seventeen bedrooms and ten bathrooms, three floors, four panic rooms, an underground tunnel, and a backyard full of weed plants.

"Two outside. We just going to back in and carry all the drugs out in bags," Force stated, climbing out of the driver's seat on some smooth shit.

Tat-tat-tat-tat-tat-tat-tat-tat!

Force and Demon crushed the two Jamaicans standing in the front. They slid in the house to see a couple of guards with headphones on, dancing like they were at a Sean Paul concert.

Tat-tat-tat-tat-tat-tat-tat!

Guards come from upstairs firing at Force and Demon as they were cleaning house, leaving bodies everywhere, making their way up to dodge bullets.

Demon felt a bullet hit his vest, almost knocking him back down the stairs. "Shittt!" Demon yelled.

Tat-tat-tat-tat-tat-tat-tat-tat!

Force killed the last three dread heads upstairs. One body flipped over the railing, falling three flights.

"Stop crying, nigga. Come on, this the room right here," Force said, opening the French double doors leading into the bedroom.

"This is the big dresser," Demon stated.

"This shit looks like a china cabinet," Force replied, trying to move it by himself. "Nigga, you just gonna stand there until they come back?" Force yelled.

Demon helped him the best he could, but he was in pain from getting shot in the vest. When they moved it off the wall, they saw a door with a punch-in code. Karol had told Demon the code. He punched it in and the door popped open. There was an elevator.

"Come on. Let's get to the prize," Force said, pumped up, getting inside the elevator and closing the door behind them, going to the underground part of the mansion. The tunnel was dim, but there was a room at the end of the hall.

"She wasn't lying, bro. I told you, Karol the real deal, son. You gotta believe me sometimes," Demon said, walking down the long tunnel with red dirt as walls.

Force opened the wood door, ready to shoot, thinking some Jamaicans were going to pop out from the ceiling or from behind the door.

"Wow, son," Force said, looking around the room at all the bricks surrounding them. The room was filled with tons of coke worth billions of dollars.

"Let me look at this shit," Demon said, taking a brick from the stack that was taller than him, going around the room.

"You hear that noise?" Force asked, hearing a ticking sound.

Demon heard it too. Both men looked around the room and found the noise was coming from behind the brick near the door.

Force moved the bricks to see a large ticking bomb counting down to five seconds.

"Demon, it's over."

"Huh?"

Boom!

The place blew up. The vibration could be heard from blocks away. Force and Demon were blown to pieces.

***

Brooklyn, NY

Karol was in her condo on the phone with Mad Max's parents. They were thanking her for finding their son's killer - or so they thought, because that's what Karol told them. When she hung up, she started laughing so hard tears formed in her eyes.

Karol used Force and Demon to gain a new plug. Mad Max's parents promised her keys at a low price. She couldn't refuse that, so she sent Force and Demon into a rabbit trap and it worked so well that she wanted to give herself a pat on her back.

The maid opened the front door to do her daily job, but Karol had her back to her, so she didn't see Wolf behind her with his gun to the maid back.

Boc! Boc!

Karol turned around in the living room after hearing the gunshots and saw her house maid fall face first into the floor with two bullets to her dome. Karol got up and rushed to the AK-47 next to her fireplace.

Boc! Boc! Boc!

Wolf shot her fake leg off, making her fall on the table, breaking the glass.

"Ahhhhhhhh, fuck!" she yelled.

"You're Jimenez's daughter? You're cute for a handicapped bitch."

"Fuck you."

"If you had legs, I would. You're very smart, but I know all about you. Before I killed your father, I was going to kill you first, but I couldn't bring myself to do it"

"Too bad."

"I'm here now, Karol."

Boc! Boc! Boc! Boc! Boc! Boc! Boc! Boc!

Wolf continued to shoot the Glock 27 until it was empty. He had been waiting on Karol for a while now and when he got the news of Andy being killed by vicious dog bites, he knew who was responsible. Wolf knew Karol had dogs in Yonkers and all over the city. She was into dog fighting. That's how he found out about her.

Wolf had a flight to catch in an hour so he left, thinking about his son's death. When he got the news about Salma and his son, he felt like the world was snatched from under his feet.

***

Hollywood Hills, Cali

Paola was in her hot bubble bath, singing songs from a Rihanna album. She was happy to be home and back in her comfort zone because New York was too much stress.

Business was doing well in Cali. She was making millions in days. She was thinking about building a new Five Families era, but she needed the right people she could trust. Paola also had ties to the Mexican Cartel in Mexico so she was on top of the world.

She got out of the tube, grabbing a towel, drying herself off. She had been exercising heavily lately and her body was in tip top shape. Walking out of the bathroom, she saw Wolf standing there with a vicious look.

"Romeo——"

Boc!

"Ahhhhh!" Wolf had shot Paola in the foot. She fell on the ground trying to stop the bleeding by holding her foot.

Boc!

Wolf shot her in the left hand. Hearing her cry in pain was like music to his ears

"You killed my son."

"So what, Romeo? You gave that bitch a seed and not me!" she screamed

"You tried to kill me. How could I?"

"I got news for you, bitch. I'm pregnant!" she yelled.

"That line won't save you today, love."

"I don't care. Kill me. I have nothing to live for, but more to die for," she said in pain, trying to stop the bleeding.

"I love you, Paola. I hate that it has to end like this."

"Save your speech for another bitch," Paola said, not trying to hear what he had to say.

Wolf emptied his clip into her, firing shot after shot, leaving blood all over the place. The guards were all dead downstairs, so he walked out the front door with his calm demeanor, thinking about his next mission, which was in Costa Rica. Everything Wolf loved was now dead. He was heartless now, and he knew how the lonely wolf felt.

***

Auburn Maximum Security Prison, NY

OG Chuck was in the prison meal hall eating dinner with other convicts talking about sports and rappers, but OG paid them no mind.

When the clock hit six p.m. on the dot, a prisoner stood up from his table, which was against the rules. Once you sat down, you had to stay seated until a C.O. told you to get up.

"Ayeee, you, sit the fuck down!" a big white guard yelled, pulling on a baton, about to hit the young black man from OG's tier on D-Block.

When the guard hit the black man with the hard stick, the place went up into a big uproar. A riot took place. Inmates started fucking up guards as the riot team came in. OG Chuck punched a guard in his face, knocking him out and going in his pockets, taking his keys and ID. OG ran into a private closet where a riot uniform awaited him.

OG got dressed and stormed out into the chaos, exiting the kitchen to see more riot guards and C.O.s rushing to the kitchen. A young Spanish female C.O. stopped OG and looked at him, seeing he was holding his arm as if he was hurt.

"Let me help you. EMS should be outside," she said, helping him towards the front of the jail. "We have an officer hurt!" the female C.O. said, stopping at closed metal doors.

There were correctional officers behind the mirrors not trying to let anybody out, but they had a hurt officer, so they opened the door, not even looking at the man under the helmet. He flashed his ID and that was good enough.

Police, fire fighters, and EMS workers were running into the prison. Ten guards were already dead and twelve prisoners were dead also.

"You good?" the beautiful guard asked. She was a rookie and on her third day on the job.

"Yeah," OG said, taking off his helmet, kissing her soft lips. "Let's go," OG Chuck told his wife Maryanna.

They got in her BMW, racing off as far away from the Watertown area as they could get. OG Chuck had been planning this day for years. The schoolteacher had placed a riot gear uniform in the meal hall closet earlier that day. He paid her $500,000 to do it. He had been fucking the young schoolteacher for years before CB started fucking her.

OG Chuck was half Cuban and Black, but his brother was a boss in Cuba and Chuck was under him. He had been married to Maryanna for ten years now. She had been in his life since he took her V-card. He had her kill his DA, his judge in Liberty, his arresting officer the night he was arrested in Brooklyn, and his lawyer who fucked him over. Maryanna was his ride or die. She had played her cards correct. He made her train Wolf as a kid so he could become the man who he was today.

"We have a lot to talk about on the flight to Cuba, and you won't be happy, papi," Maryanna said.

"What else is new? But now that I'm back, a lot of things are about to change and a lot of blood is about to be spilled," OG Chuck stated, staring into the mountains out his window.

To Be Continued in
Kingpins: La Familia

Killers on Elm Street 3

Coming Soon

Romell Tukes

Submission Guideline

Submit the first three chapters of your completed manuscript to ldpsubmissions@gmail.com, subject line: Your book's title. The manuscript must be in a .doc file and sent as an attachment. Document should be in Times New Roman, double spaced and in size 12 font. Also, provide your synopsis and full contact information. If sending multiple submissions, they must each be in a separate email.

Have a story but no way to send it electronically? You can still submit to LDP/Ca$h Presents. Send in the first three chapters, written or typed, of your completed manuscript to:

LDP: Submissions Dept
Po Box 944
Stockbridge, Ga 30281

DO NOT send original manuscript. Must be a duplicate.

Provide your synopsis and a cover letter containing your full contact information.

Thanks for considering LDP and Ca$h Presents.

Romell Tukes

Coming Soon from Lock Down Publications/Ca$h Presents

BOW DOWN TO MY GANGSTA

By **Ca$h**

TORN BETWEEN TWO

By **Coffee**

THE STREETS STAINED MY SOUL **II**

By **Marcellus Allen**

BLOOD OF A BOSS **VI**

SHADOWS OF THE GAME II

TRAP BASTARD II

By **Askari**

LOYAL TO THE GAME **IV**

By **T.J. & Jelissa**

IF LOVING YOU IS WRONG... **III**

By **Jelissa**

TRUE SAVAGE **VIII**

MIDNIGHT CARTEL IV

DOPE BOY MAGIC IV

CITY OF KINGZ III

By **Chris Green**

BLAST FOR ME **III**

A SAVAGE DOPEBOY III

CUTTHROAT MAFIA III

DUFFLE BAG CARTEL VI

HEARTLESS GOON VI

By **Ghost**

A HUSTLER'S DECEIT III

KILL ZONE **II**

BAE BELONGS TO ME III

A DOPE BOY'S QUEEN III

By **Aryanna**

COKE KINGS V

KING OF THE TRAP III

By **T.J. Edwards**

GORILLAZ IN THE BAY V

3X KRAZY III

De'Kari

THE STREETS ARE CALLING II

Duquie Wilson

KINGPIN KILLAZ IV

STREET KINGS III

PAID IN BLOOD III

CARTEL KILLAZ IV

DOPE GODS III

Hood Rich

SINS OF A HUSTLA II

ASAD

KINGZ OF THE GAME VI

Playa Ray

SLAUGHTER GANG IV

RUTHLESS HEART IV

By Willie Slaughter

FUK SHYT II

By Blakk Diamond

TRAP QUEEN

RICH $AVAGE II

By Troublesome

YAYO V

GHOST MOB II

Stilloan Robinson
CREAM III
By Yolanda Moore
SON OF A DOPE FIEND III
HEAVEN GOT A GHETTO II
By Renta
FOREVER GANGSTA II
GLOCKS ON SATIN SHEETS III
By Adrian Dulan
LOYALTY AIN'T PROMISED III
By Keith Williams
THE PRICE YOU PAY FOR LOVE III
By Destiny Skai
I'M NOTHING WITHOUT HIS LOVE II
SINS OF A THUG II
TO THE THUG I LOVED BEFORE II
By Monet Dragun
LIFE OF A SAVAGE IV
MURDA SEASON IV
GANGLAND CARTEL IV
CHI'RAQ GANGSTAS IV
KILLERS ON ELM STREET IV
JACK BOYZ N DA BRONX II
A DOPEBOY'S DREAM II
By **Romell Tukes**
QUIET MONEY IV
EXTENDED CLIP III
THUG LIFE IV
By **Trai'Quan**

Romell Tukes

THE STREETS MADE ME III

By **Larry D. Wright**

IF YOU CROSS ME ONCE II

ANGEL III

By **Anthony Fields**

FRIEND OR FOE III

By **Mimi**

SAVAGE STORMS III

By **Meesha**

BLOOD ON THE MONEY III

By J-Blunt

THE STREETS WILL NEVER CLOSE II

By K'ajji

NIGHTMARES OF A HUSTLA III

By King Dream

IN THE ARM OF HIS BOSS

By Jamila

HARD AND RUTHLESS III

MOB TOWN 251 II

By Von Diesel

LEVELS TO THIS SHYT II

By Ah'Million

MOB TIES III

By SayNoMore

BODYMORE MURDERLAND II

By Delmont Player

THE LAST OF THE OGS III

Tranay Adams

FOR THE LOVE OF A BOSS II

By C. D. Blue

Available Now

RESTRAINING ORDER **I & II**

By **CA$H & Coffee**

LOVE KNOWS NO BOUNDARIES **I II & III**

By **Coffee**

RAISED AS A GOON I, II, III & IV

BRED BY THE SLUMS I, II, III

BLAST FOR ME I & II

ROTTEN TO THE CORE I II III

A BRONX TALE I, II, III

DUFFLE BAG CARTEL I II III IV V

HEARTLESS GOON I II III IV V

A SAVAGE DOPEBOY I II

DRUG LORDS I II III

CUTTHROAT MAFIA I II

By **Ghost**

LAY IT DOWN **I & II**

LAST OF A DYING BREED I II

BLOOD STAINS OF A SHOTTA I & II III

By **Jamaica**

LOYAL TO THE GAME I II III

LIFE OF SIN I, II III

By **TJ & Jelissa**

BLOODY COMMAS I & II

SKI MASK CARTEL I II & III

KING OF NEW YORK I II,III IV V

Romell Tukes

RISE TO POWER I II III

COKE KINGS I II III IV

BORN HEARTLESS I II III IV

KING OF THE TRAP I II

By **T.J. Edwards**

IF LOVING HIM IS WRONG...I & II

LOVE ME EVEN WHEN IT HURTS I II III

By **Jelissa**

WHEN THE STREETS CLAP BACK I & II III

THE HEART OF A SAVAGE I II III

By **Jibril Williams**

A DISTINGUISHED THUG STOLE MY HEART I II & III

LOVE SHOULDN'T HURT I II III IV

RENEGADE BOYS I II III IV

PAID IN KARMA I II III

SAVAGE STORMS I II

By **Meesha**

A GANGSTER'S CODE I &, II III

A GANGSTER'S SYN I II III

THE SAVAGE LIFE I II III

CHAINED TO THE STREETS I II III

BLOOD ON THE MONEY I II

By **J-Blunt**

PUSH IT TO THE LIMIT

By **Bre' Hayes**

BLOOD OF A BOSS **I, II, III, IV, V**

SHADOWS OF THE GAME

TRAP BASTARD

By **Askari**

THE STREETS BLEED MURDER **I, II & III**

190

THE HEART OF A GANGSTA I II& III

By **Jerry Jackson**

CUM FOR ME I II III IV V VI VII

An **LDP Erotica Collaboration**

BRIDE OF A HUSTLA **I II & II**

THE FETTI GIRLS **I, II& III**

CORRUPTED BY A GANGSTA I, II III, IV

BLINDED BY HIS LOVE

THE PRICE YOU PAY FOR LOVE I II

DOPE GIRL MAGIC I II III

By **Destiny Skai**

WHEN A GOOD GIRL GOES BAD

By **Adrienne**

THE COST OF LOYALTY I II III

By Kweli

A GANGSTER'S REVENGE **I II III & IV**

THE BOSS MAN'S DAUGHTERS I II III IV V

A SAVAGE LOVE **I & II**

BAE BELONGS TO ME I II

A HUSTLER'S DECEIT I, II, III

WHAT BAD BITCHES DO I, II, III

SOUL OF A MONSTER I II III

KILL ZONE

A DOPE BOY'S QUEEN I II

By **Aryanna**

A KINGPIN'S AMBITON

A KINGPIN'S AMBITION **II**

I MURDER FOR THE DOUGH

By **Ambitious**

TRUE SAVAGE I II III IV V VI VII

DOPE BOY MAGIC I, II, III
MIDNIGHT CARTEL I II III
CITY OF KINGZ I II
By **Chris Green**
A DOPEBOY'S PRAYER
By **Eddie "Wolf" Lee**
THE KING CARTEL **I, II & III**
By **Frank Gresham**
THESE NIGGAS AIN'T LOYAL **I, II & III**
By **Nikki Tee**
GANGSTA SHYT **I II &III**
By **CATO**
THE ULTIMATE BETRAYAL
By **Phoenix**
BOSS'N UP **I , II & III**
By **Royal Nicole**
I LOVE YOU TO DEATH
By Destiny J
I RIDE FOR MY HITTA
I STILL RIDE FOR MY HITTA
By **Misty Holt**
LOVE & CHASIN' PAPER
By **Qay Crockett**
TO DIE IN VAIN
SINS OF A HUSTLA
By **ASAD**
BROOKLYN HUSTLAZ
By **Boogsy Morina**
BROOKLYN ON LOCK I & II
By **Sonovia**

GANGSTA CITY

By **Teddy Duke**

A DRUG KING AND HIS DIAMOND I & II III

A DOPEMAN'S RICHES

HER MAN, MINE'S TOO I, II

CASH MONEY HO'S

THE WIFEY I USED TO BE I II

By Nicole Goosby

TRAPHOUSE KING **I II & III**

KINGPIN KILLAZ I II III

STREET KINGS I II

PAID IN BLOOD **I II**

CARTEL KILLAZ I II III

DOPE GODS I II

By **Hood Rich**

LIPSTICK KILLAH **I, II, III**

CRIME OF PASSION I II & III

FRIEND OR FOE I II

By **Mimi**

STEADY MOBBN' **I, II, III**

THE STREETS STAINED MY SOUL

By **Marcellus Allen**

WHO SHOT YA **I, II, III**

SON OF A DOPE FIEND I II

HEAVEN GOT A GHETTO

Renta

GORILLAZ IN THE BAY **I II III IV**

TEARS OF A GANGSTA I II

3X KRAZY I II

DE'KARI

TRIGGADALE I II III

Elijah R. Freeman

GOD BLESS THE TRAPPERS I, II, III

THESE SCANDALOUS STREETS I, II, III

FEAR MY GANGSTA I, II, III IV, V

THESE STREETS DON'T LOVE NOBODY I, II

BURY ME A G I, II, III, IV, V

A GANGSTA'S EMPIRE I, II, III, IV

THE DOPEMAN'S BODYGAURD I II

THE REALEST KILLAZ I II III

THE LAST OF THE OGS I II

Tranay Adams

THE STREETS ARE CALLING

Duquie Wilson

MARRIED TO A BOSS... I II III

By Destiny Skai & Chris Green

KINGZ OF THE GAME I II III IV V

Playa Ray

SLAUGHTER GANG I II III

RUTHLESS HEART I II III

By Willie Slaughter

FUK SHYT

By Blakk Diamond

DON'T F#CK WITH MY HEART I II

By Linnea

ADDICTED TO THE DRAMA I II III

IN THE ARM OF HIS BOSS II

By Jamila

YAYO I II III IV

A SHOOTER'S AMBITION I II

By S. Allen
TRAP GOD I II III
RICH $AVAGE
By Troublesome
FOREVER GANGSTA
GLOCKS ON SATIN SHEETS I II
By Adrian Dulan
TOE TAGZ I II III
LEVELS TO THIS SHYT
By Ah'Million
KINGPIN DREAMS I II III
By Paper Boi Rari
CONFESSIONS OF A GANGSTA I II III
By Nicholas Lock
I'M NOTHING WITHOUT HIS LOVE
SINS OF A THUG
TO THE THUG I LOVED BEFORE
By Monet Dragun
CAUGHT UP IN THE LIFE I II III
By Robert Baptiste
NEW TO THE GAME I II III
MONEY, MURDER & MEMORIES I II III
By **Malik D. Rice**
LIFE OF A SAVAGE I II III
A GANGSTA'S QUR'AN I II III
MURDA SEASON I II III
GANGLAND CARTEL I II III
CHI'RAQ GANGSTAS I II III
KILLERS ON ELM STREET I II III

JACK BOYZ N DA BRONX

A DOPEBOY'S DREAM

By **Romell Tukes**

LOYALTY AIN'T PROMISED I II

By Keith Williams

QUIET MONEY I II III

THUG LIFE I II III

EXTENDED CLIP I II

By **Trai'Quan**

THE STREETS MADE ME I II

By **Larry D. Wright**

THE ULTIMATE SACRIFICE I, II, III, IV, V, VI

KHADIFI

IF YOU CROSS ME ONCE

ANGEL I II

By **Anthony Fields**

THE LIFE OF A HOOD STAR

By Ca$h & Rashia Wilson

THE STREETS WILL NEVER CLOSE

By K'ajji

CREAM I II

By Yolanda Moore

NIGHTMARES OF A HUSTLA I II

By King Dream

CONCRETE KILLA I II

By Kingpen

HARD AND RUTHLESS I II

MOB TOWN 251

By Von Diesel

GHOST MOB II

Stilloan Robinson

MOB TIES I II

By SayNoMore

BODYMORE MURDERLAND

By Delmont Player

FOR THE LOVE OF A BOSS

By C. D. Blue

BOOKS BY LDP'S CEO, CA$H

TRUST IN NO MAN

TRUST IN NO MAN 2

TRUST IN NO MAN 3

BONDED BY BLOOD

SHORTY GOT A THUG

THUGS CRY

THUGS CRY 2

THUGS CRY 3

TRUST NO BITCH

TRUST NO BITCH 2

TRUST NO BITCH 3

TIL MY CASKET DROPS

RESTRAINING ORDER

RESTRAINING ORDER 2

IN LOVE WITH A CONVICT

LIFE OF A HOOD STAR

Killers on Elm Street 3

CPSIA information can be obtained
at www.ICGtesting.com
Printed in the USA
LVHW020025110921
697560LV00017B/1523